The author is a chartered engineer and has worked and travelled extensively in Asia. His interest in writing sprang from the many technical papers he wrote for the technical journals of his industry. Although, originally from Newcastle upon Tyne, he has lived in South Wales with his wife and three children for many years.

To my wife, Sylvia.
The nicest person I know.

John Pimley

HACKER

AUSTIN MACAULEY PUBLISHERS™

LONDON · CAMBRIDGE · NEW YORK · SHARJAH

A CIP catalogue record for this title is available from the British Library.

ISBN 9781528920087 (Paperback)
ISBN 9781528962971 (ePub e-book)

www.austinmacauley.com

First Published (2020)
Austin Macauley Publishers Ltd
25 Canada Square
Canary Wharf
London
E14 5LQ

Chapter 1

When Mike was asked why he was a Hacker, he always said he felt that he was improving ordinary people's security by showing how poor the banks and other organisations were at protecting the information they had stored. He also commented that it was up to these institutions to improve their security and they should be thanking him for showing them the error of their ways, or that is what he thought until he went one step too far. Then his life disintegrated.

He had become bored with the usual "let's infiltrate this bank or that bank or some government department." He thought there must be something more testing. So delving deeper into coding and looking way beyond the normal level he found a strange anomaly; in fact, he found evidence of another type of programming language that was infiltrating the languages normally used. He could not 'read' what this odd code was saying, but it was clear that it entered our all the codes he was acquainted with unhampered and bypassed all the security blocks that were present.

Who was writing this code? Was it an enemy nation? That was unlikely as he was knowledgeable about their infiltration methods from his early days at GCHQ and he would have recognised them.

Little headway was made even after working steadily for months trying to decipher this strange language as the whole basis of its design was way beyond anything he had seen before. Then one day, his life changed as he sat at the computer tapping away trying another angle to enter the code and actually making some progress. Suddenly, the computer screen went blank and as he looked at it, it seemed as if he was staring into a void. It also seemed to be drawing him towards the screen. At that moment, his phone rang and luckily, it was almost out of reach, as he leant over to reach it the computer screen exploded. Razor-sharp material from the screen rocketed past him through the exact location his head had been a fraction of a second earlier. When he looked at the parts of the screen embedded in the wall behind him, he knew that if he had not moved, then the debris would have killed him. How did it happen? Why did it happen? He had never even heard of a computer exploding. To say he was shaken up would be an understatement.

Realising that the phone was still ringing, he shakily picked it up from where it had fallen. Before he could ask who was calling, a female voice screamed, "Get away from your computer. They are on to you. If you want to survive, meet me at 2 p.m. which is in two hours' time at the place where you and your band first played music in public. Disguise yourself and walk there, don't use public transport, don't use your phone again and don't carry it with you." She then ended the call.

Mike's mind was still struggling with his closeness to death, so he did not to even try to comprehend the 'how and the why' of the message. He sat there stunned for quite a while.

Slowly as his mind recovered, He realised that the telephone call implied that the explosion was not a freak accident, but intentional. *But who was the caller? How did she know him? Who are the 'they' that are supposedly onto him? He was baffled. Also, how does she know about his playing in a band? That was when he was in his mid-teen years and apart from the other band members it was hard to image anyone else making a connection to the spot where they first played.*

Should he meet with her? He asked himself. *Is it safe? If the mysterious 'they' felt, they needed a backup plan to kill him then the proposed meeting might be part of that plan. His mind was in a whirl.*

He slowly concluded that he had to attend the meeting, otherwise he would be completely in the dark as to what was happening to him. To be safe, he decided to arrive at the meeting place early and watch what was happening. He hurriedly put on a hoody, a cap to cover part of his face and dark glasses. Hoping he was suitably disguised, he slipped out the back door, scaled the fence at the back of the house and started walking to the location of his musical debut. Luckily, the route he took passed along a tree-lined path which he hoped would shield him from prying eyes. After 30 minutes, he entered the local park and approached the rendezvous which was an arena with a stage which had not been used for the last 15 to 20 years and was now derelict. He kept in the shadow of the trees and carefully examined the surrounding area; it was deserted. Tucking himself behind a bush, he waited and watched. The appointed meeting time came and went without a sight of anyone. After another 30 minutes frustration set-in and he left the shelter of the bush and approached the stage.

It was in poor shape and was avoided by most people. He then noticed what looked like a new paper envelope lying in the centre of its broken-down floor. He carefully made his way across the floor not only avoiding the more seriously damaged parts of the floor but also looking out for what could be a trap. As he got closer, he could see that the envelope was addressed to him. He gingerly lifted the envelope and retreated behind the bush. *What was going on? Why all this cloak-and-dagger stuff?* He asked himself.

He carefully opened the envelope ensuring nothing nasty was going to pop out. Inside was a note and a coach ticket to a small village some 30 miles away. The note said,

Wear a disguise. Put a stone in one of your shoes to give you a credible limp as you walk to the coach station. Use the coach ticket. Upon arrival, put the stone in your other shoe, leave the coach station and walk to the address given below, carefully following the route shown on the sketched map. Avoid cameras. Do not carry or use a phone. Do not use a credit card. We will meet you there.

The note was signed, *The Sentinel.*

What had he gotten himself into? He began to think it was a practical joke until he remembered the exploding computer screen, which convinced him, whether he liked it or not, that he had to follow the instructions.

Chapter 2

The stone certainly produced a limp as he walked to the Central Coach Station. He wondered if his foot would ever recover and hoped the pain, he was going through was for a good reason.

Mike boarded the coach without incident and spent the journey trying to put a logical reason to the incident that had almost killed him. It seemed that whoever was infiltrating the computer systems had caused the explosion. But even with his experience of programming, he could not see how they could possibly do it.

He alighted from the coach then switched the stone to his other shoe. He then followed the route shown on the map. This led him through the least populated parts of the village and up to a cottage surrounded by trees. He thought, as he took the stone out of his shoe, *in time, he may forget this journey, but his feet would remember it.*

He hesitated as he looked at the cottage. There was no sign of life outside and he wondered what awaited him in there.

The door of the cottage opened, and a young woman beckoned to him. "Please come in. I have been waiting for you," she said with a wide smile on her face.

He noted, she only said, "she" and not "they"; maybe she was the only one there. He felt a little safer.

Mike approached and entered the cottage.

He was directed to what would be the living room. It had basic furnishings; a settee, two chairs and a table.

"My name is Amy and yours, I believe, is Mike. I see you are thinking that this place hardly looks lived-in, and you are correct," Amy said as she gestured for him to sit down. "We only use this place to meet and interview newcomers."

"Interview?" He said. "I am not applying for a job. I thought you could help explain what has happened to cause my computer to explode. Your phone call intimated you could help."

"Your computer exploded?" She asked, her face registering shock. "We did not realise they were so advanced. To generate that amount of energy is astounding and frightening. All we expected was that they would warn you off by frying your computer drive in front of your eyes. It seems things are worse that we feared."

"Well, that was what happened and to repeat myself, can you help?" He asked rather crossly.

"Yes, we can. But we must know about you," she replied sharply. Whilst you have had a terrible experience, you are not the only one who has had their life put at risk. In fact, everyone in our group is in the same boat as you, and for us to be safe, we have to be sure that you are who you say you are and that you are on the level."

"OK. What do you want to know?" He asked impatiently.

"What was the name of your first dog?"

"What?" He asked

"What was the name of your first dog?" She asked again more firmly.

"It was Rex. But how the hell would you be able to check that? I could say anything," he answered angrily.

"Yes, Rex is correct, and 'No' you could not say anything," she answered, with a steely glint in her eyes. "Do you think we are stupid? Do you think we would ask you questions which could be answered by someone who has recently accessed your computer? We have delved into parts of your life long before you became a hacker. We want to help you, but we are not going to risk our security. So, either accept us as we are or leave," she added, pointing to the door.

Mike was taken aback by the change in her demeanour. From the gentle-looking girl who met me, she had changed into someone you would not like to cross.

He thought her change in attitude must have been reflected in his face, as she now adopted her earlier look. She smiled and said, "I want you to know we are serious. We think you could be of great help to us, but we have to know whether you are serious too."

"OK, I apologise for my earlier attitude. Fire away. Ask what you want," he replied, with his hands in front of himself in a placating manner.

The questions she asked astounded him. They dealt with aspects of his life that he had almost forgotten about. He must have answered correctly as after about 30 minutes, she said, "OK, that should do it. Welcome to the Sentinels."

"Now it's my turn," he said. "Firstly, what are the Sentinels?"

"We are a group of people who have been put at risk by a mysterious country or organisation which can infiltrate our lives electronically with impunity. We have tried to fight back but their spread of influence throughout the electronic systems has defeated us," she answered.

"OK, but how do you think I can help. Whatever it is has nearly killed me, so I wonder if I am any better than your group," he asked.

"We have been watching you. You came to our attention during our attempts to find out what was behind all the attacks on us. Although our programming knowledge is not up to your standard, we were able break into your computer and we could see that you were very much more advanced than us," she said.

"So, you broke into my computer?" He said with a laugh. "The hacker got hacked."

"Yes, we have been watching your advances in penetrating the programme interloper. Then we noticed a huge increase in their output, and it seemed to be directed at your network address, hence my telephone call to you."

"Well, you saved my life and I am indebted to you," he responded with feeling.

"You are welcome," she said, smiling.

"So, if I am now part of the Sentinels, what happens now?" He asked.

"We leave here and travel to our headquarters," she replied, as she started to put her coat on.

"Wow, there is no hanging-about then," he commented with a smile on his face.

"Let's see if you continue smiling," she said with a laugh as she opened a cupboard and took out two cycle helmets.

The smile did drop off his face. "Cycling? I haven't cycled in twenty years."

"Well, you know what they say, 'you never forget how to ride a bike'," she said with another laugh, as she thrust the helmet into his hands. "But it won't be too bad as they are electric, so at least your legs won't let you down," she added as she went out of the cottage door.

He followed her out of the cottage. She then locked the cottage door and led him up to a small shed at the rear of the cottage. She entered the shed and pushed a bicycle out saying, "This is yours." She then came out of the shed with a similar bicycle which she expertly mounted and started riding off down the road. "Aren't you coming?" she shouted over her shoulder.

He mounted the bike and started pedalling quickly to catch up to her. "Remember, I have not ridden for ages and I have no knowledge of how an electric bike works," he said, as he caught up to her.

"What! An electronic genius like you doesn't know how to work a simple electric switch. I am surprised!" she shouted at him, then with a big smile on her face she accelerated away ahead of him.

He could hear her laughter as he tried to find the correct switch to tweak.

Eventually he found it, engaged the electric motor and pedalling as fast as he could, he caught up with her. "You're crazy," he said with a big grin on his face.

"Yes, and I am faster than you," she replied as she again accelerated away from him.

When he caught up with her again, she wiped her brow with the back of her hand and said, "Phew, that's as much fun as I have had in a long time. I think we can slow down now, as we have quite a distance to go."

She was correct, as they rode steadily for another hour taking backroads and lanes until they reached what looked like a Nissan Hut.

"Is this it?" He asked in a surprised manner.

"Yes, it is," she replied sharply, as she dismounted from her bicycle. "What did you expect, a multi-storeyed office building? We are on the run. We don't have a lot of money and it suits us perfectly."

"I apologise," he said. "I didn't mean to sound insulting. I did not expect an office complex, but I thought it might be a proper building."

"You have to realise that we have to be protected from whatever is attacking us via every type of communication device. Other than electricity, this building has no connection with the world at large and even the electricity usage is not registered."

"So, in other words, you are stealing the electricity," he answered.

"Yes, however, our main aim is not to rob the electricity generating company, but to keep our identities and location a secret," she responded with vigour.

"OK. You have managed to hide successfully, but how are you fighting back?" He asked pointedly.

"Maybe you should come inside, meet our team, and I will let them answer that question," she said as she walked towards the hut entrance.

He entered the hut and was pleasantly surprised. It had obviously been divided into several rooms judging by the internal walls and doors that he could see. The room they entered appeared to be the living area which was furnished with plenty of comfortable-looking chairs, several small tables and a huge television. Three men and one woman occupied four of the chairs, casually watching television. They looked up as they both entered the room.

"Hi," one of them said to Amy, "I see you got him!"

"Yes, and just in time," Amy replied.

"What do you mean, just in time?" The girl asked.

"They exploded his computer. He is lucky to be alive," Amy said.

"Surely, you are joking. How the hell could they explode his computer?" One of the men asked.

"I wish we knew," Amy answered. "But it happened. The Controller has just moved up its attacks to a new level and I think we are in more danger. Instead of just limiting our lives this thing is willing to kill us."

"So, what do you think, Mike?" One of the men asked, skewing his chair around to face him. "Do you think they tried to kill you?"

"Absolutely," he replied. "There is no doubt. It, or the Controller as you call it, set a trap and it was only Amy's phone call that saved me." He then went on to explain in detail what happened.

There was silence after he finished, with the group looking at each other with worried looks on their faces.

Rising from their chairs, they introduced themselves. The first was a girl called Greta. She was a thin, intense-looking girl of around 25 years old. She had long black hair done into a ponytail. She wore tight jeans and a striped top. She greeted him with a big smile and said how pleased she was that he had decided to join them. He did not comment on the fact that the jury was still out on whether he joined them or not. The next person was a man who introduced himself as Phil. He seemed a quiet studious type who, although shook Mike's hand warmly, he did not make eye contact, which Mike hoped, was due to shyness rather than negativity. He was quite tall and thin, slightly balding with mousey hair. He was dressed in jeans and a white shirt worn outside the jeans. Next was Joe. He was of an average height with a muscular build and a bone-crushing handshake. He again wore jeans and a shirt worn outside the jeans. He made strong eye contact and welcomed him with a big smile. Finally, there was Mark. He was tall with blonde hair and a beard. He did not seem too keen to see Mike and whilst he shook his hand, his greeting was restricted to 'Hi' before he turned away and regained his seat. He again wore jeans and shirt.

What was he to make of the crew? Now that we were introduced. He thought I better find out.

"Well," he said. "You know more about me than I know about you. So, would you each give me a little history on why you find yourselves here?"

They looked at each other. Mark slumped back in his chair. Joe twisted his face. Phil looked positive but it was Greta who turned to him and said, "I am, or rather I was, a control engineer for the Electricity Board. My problems began when I noticed anomalies in some of the requests for power coming from a certain area. The demands were well above historical levels; also, a check on the electrical infrastructure questioned whether the cabling etc. could carry the load. So, as the area was reasonably close to where I lived, I decided to visit it. The place was not a factory, but the power requested was such that one would expect high-energy-using equipment. Back at the office I made enquires via the Internet about the location. That was my mistake. My life then fell apart. Next thing was all my credit cards were cancelled. I spoke to the bank who said I had cancelled them. My direct debits were cancelled. My telephone, electricity, gas and mobile phone were all cut off. Again, enquires indicated that I had requested them all to be cancelled. Then my manager called me in to tell me I was instantly dismissed for attempting to reduce the cost of the consumed power supplied to my friends. I argued and he then showed me the charts and figures which did indicate someone had been tampering with the figures and the trail led back to my computer. I denied all knowledge but was escorted from the building with the warning that any other complaints would lead to criminal proceedings being taken against me." Greta's eyes filled with tears at this point and she could not continue speaking. Even though we did not really know each other, Mike put his arms around her, thanked her, and guided her back to her seat.

Turning to the others and shaking his head in sympathy, he said, "Wow. Beat that!"

"I don't know about beating it," Joe said, as he turned his chair towards him. "But I have a similar story. I was a policeman, in fact a detective. I was given a case about two men found electrocuted, but there was no electrical source near where the bodies were found. As I investigated their history, I found that they were known burglars with plenty of convictions. In truth they were small-time in as much as they broke into industrial premises stealing tools and any saleable things they found. They had a van which I eventually tracked down. It was parked close to a business park. I began to think that someone on the park had possibly opened their premises and found the two bodies and moved them as they did not want the hassle associated with informing the police, or maybe they had something to hide. I then made the same mistake as Greta and used the computer to investigate the various businesses on the estate. Within days I was arrested for corruption. Apparently, I was receiving money from a known mobster; this money having been paid into my bank account. I explained to them that if I was on the 'take' would I make it so obvious? This made them pause and they decided to drop the corruption charge, but I was dismissed from the force immediately." With this, Joe sat down and said, "Next!"

Phil looked at Mark, who showed no interest in moving so Phil stood up and said, "I was a lecturer at a local college. I have an interest in programming, not up to your standard I hasten to add, but enough to see anomalies occurring. I started to investigate but did not seem to make much headway, but obviously sufficient to alert whoever is behind the oddities, because I was called into the principal's office and shown vile photographs which were stored on my computer at the college. I of course denied any knowledge of them. They said that is what they expected me to say and I was fired and immediately escorted from the college." Phil's hands were shaking as he related his story so Mike patted him on the shoulder and shook his head in sorrow as Phil returned to his seat.

"So, what is your story, Mark?" Mike asked.

"Similar, that's all you need to know," he replied as he slumped back in his chair.

"Are you always so negative?" Mike asked, "Or is it just with me?"

"A bit of both, but mainly you," he said aggressively, sitting forward in his chair.

"Please, please," Amy said as she moved between them. "We have to get along. We are all we have. And remember Mark, we invited him here."

"No. You four invited him here. If you remember, I abstained," Mark said with some venom. With that, he got up out of his chair and left the room.

Mike looked around bemused. "I think maybe I should leave," he said, moving towards the door.

"Please don't go," Amy said pleadingly as she grasped his arm. "We need you. You are possibly our only chance of getting our lives back."

"Thanks for that vote of confidence. But how do the rest feel?" He asked as he turned to where they were sitting.

"Ignore Mark," Joe said. "He thinks you are going to usurp him as the technical expert. He will come around."

"Stay," Phil said.

"Please stay," Greta said. Her hands pressed together as if praying.

"OK, I will give it a try. But we are going to have our hands full with this internet interloper, and internal strife is not going to help." He said, as he took a seat, hoping it was not Mark's.

"If you are totally isolated here, where do you access the Internet or do your coding?" He asked.

They looked at each other in a slightly embarrassed manner.

"We use internet café's, although we have to keep changing which ones we use to stop being locked out of the computers," Amy said.

"Have you tried the Dark Web?" He asked.

"Yes, but whatever is hounding us has tracked us down," Amy answered.

"It seems that you are not having much success using computers, so have you checked-out the units in the business parks which caused you so much grief?" He asked

"Yes, as much as we could. Mark carried out that investigation. He found that the building was impenetrable. Also, he noticed that no one seemed to work there."

An alarm bell rang in his head. "So, he is saying with no one on guard it is still impossible to get inside the building?"

"That's what he told us," Amy said.

"Let us say that it's true." That is as far as he got before Mark burst back into the room.

"Are you calling me a liar?" He said in a threatening tone, as he strode towards Mike. He pushed Amy out of the way and made a grab for Mike. Mike swayed out of Mark's and reached out and grabbed his arm, Mike then pulled him forward and kicked his legs from underneath him. Mark went down heavily. Mike kept a hold of his arm and put his foot on Mark's throat. "Calm down, Mark. I thought we were all on the same side," he said quietly. Mark started to struggle to get up, so Mike levered Mark's arm up and put more pressure on his throat.

"If I let you up, you better behave, or I won't be so gentle next time." With that, Mike released him and stepped back out of his reach.

The rest of the group stood with open mouths.

Mark struggled to his feet, his face red, either with anger or embarrassment. He looked as though he might launch another attack, then clearly thought better of it and strode out of the room knocking Phil and Greta out of his path. The next thing that was heard was the hum of an electric bicycle motor travelling away from the building.

Amy ran to the door, looked out and said, "Mark has left."

There was a silence in the room. The group looked at each other with shock written over their faces.

"What is going to happen to our group now?" Greta asked tearfully. "I thought you joining us would improve our chances. Now I am not sure."

"I cannot apologise for what I did. I was only protecting myself," Mike said with a shake of my head. "I am willing to leave and then maybe Mark will come back."

"I was surprised at Mark's attitude," Joe said.

"Well, I am not," Phil interjected. "He had taken it upon himself to be the unelected leader and I think he saw you as a possible threat to his position."

"Well, he was wrong. Firstly, I have not decided to fully join your group, and if I did, I am not interested in being in charge," he said.

Almost as one, the group sat down and slumped back in their chairs.

"What now?" Amy said dejectedly.

"If I can make a suggestion, I think we should look at the business park units again." Mike said.

"But we told you Mark had already looked at them, and it was a no-go," Greta replied.

He did not what to publicise his doubts about Mark's report, so he said, "Maybe we don't have to enter the buildings, maybe we can sabotage the power or other feeds to them. This should bring the users hotfoot to the buildings."

"We suggested that, but Mark said he had looked and there was no visible power feed," Greta said.

More alarm bells rang in Mike's head, but again he didn't think this was the time to undermine Mark, so he suggested they have another look on the basis that Mark might have missed something and another pair of eyes might find it. This was agreed and Amy said she would accompany him to the business park.

"OK, let's go!" He said to Amy.

"Already?" She asked. "You have just got here."

"No time like the present. Have you got maps of where the business park is located? Oh, and what is its name?" He asked.

"It is called the Eastleigh Business Park," she said, as she grabbed a map together with a package from a drawer. They both got helmets and then went out to the bikes.

She said, "Wear these," and handed him a false moustache and tinted glasses. She then proceeded to put on a false nose, a wig and similar tinted glasses.

As he put the disguise on, he said to her, "Go slowly," she immediately jumped on the bike and accelerated away down the road, laughing as she went. He eventually caught her up and we settled into a steady speed along back roads until they got closer to the town. Then she gave him the map and said, "We should separate here and make our way individually. You follow the map and I will go by a different route. There are many cameras positioned in town. I know our enemy has control of them and I don't want them to see us together," with that, she rode off.

He studied the map for a few minutes, memorised the route and started cycling. After about 30 minutes of riding, he approached the business park. He dismounted some distance away from the park so that he could check out the area. After about five minutes Amy appeared on the approach road to the park. She stopped and waved to him then pointed at something over his head. He looked up to see that he was immediately under a surveillance camera. Now I could see the reason for the disguise otherwise it would have had him dead-to-rights. He cycled back to where Amy was standing and following her instructions, he lifted the cycles over a hedge to hide them from the road. They then left the road, and to avoid any cameras they made our way on foot through a field around the outside of the business park and approached the building. Even from a distance, it was clear that the building was inhabited as they saw movement through the window, also it did not look impregnable; it was just like any of other of the adjoining buildings.

"What has Mark been up to?" Amy said with a look of shock on her face. "He has told us deliberate lies."

He decided not to comment on Mark.

"Personally, I think if we wanted, we could break into that building. So why don't we go back to headquarters and decide," he suggested to Amy.

She nodded her agreement. He could see from her face that she had not recovered from Mark's deceit and was struggling to hold it together. They rode back in silence as daylight faded.

As they approach the headquarters, Amy braked suddenly and shouted, "Stop!"

He braked, drew alongside her and asked, "What is the matter?"

"Something is wrong. There are no lights showing," she said, pointing towards the headquarters.

"Maybe they are all asleep," he said.

"No," she responded. "They never go to bed this early."

"OK," he said. "Switch the bikes' lights off. Leave the bikes here and we will approach on foot."

They circled the building and approached it from the rear.

They crept closer such that they could look through a window. The place looked deserted, and the chairs and table were in disarray.

"My God! What has happened?" Amy said with shock in her voice.

"Sssh. I think there is someone hiding in that room," he said quietly.

"Oh, maybe it's them," she said, moving towards the front of the building.

He grabbed her arm. "What if it isn't them? What if it is the people who have caused the problem?"

She gulped and crouched down beside him.

"What shall we do?" she whispered.

"We have to find out more about them. Firstly, how many, secondly who they are."

"Is there a backdoor in this place?" He asked.

"Yes, along to the right, but it is usually locked," Amy said. "But when I think about it, that is the door through which Mark left, so maybe he did not bother to lock it."

He crept along the back of the building and carefully made his way up to the doorway. He tried the door and found it was unlocked. He slipped through the doorway into a narrow corridor with a few doors leading off it. He thought these must lead into the rooms He had spotted from the living area when he first entered the building earlier that day. *Which door should I open and what would I find?* He asked himself.

He chose a door and opened it carefully. It led to someone's bedroom. It was very tidy and there was a faint smell of perfume, so he assumed it belonged to either Greta or Amy. He made my way across the room and slowly and quietly opened the door a little such that he could see into the living area. The room was wrecked. Obviously, a terrific struggle had taken place.

Out of the darkness a voice complained that they had waited long enough for the missing ones to appear. He assumed they meant Amy and him. He was shocked to hear Mark's voice reply telling him to keep quiet. Mark then added that they, meaning Amy and him, had nowhere else to go and we would eventually turn up. Whilst it was no satisfaction, it seems his doubts about Mark appeared true. Another voice came out of the dark saying, "We've neutralised three of them, surely that will finish off this group. What can the other two do?"

"I want that bastard Mike. He is a real danger, plus I have something personal that I want to put right. So, shut up and wait," Mark answered with venom in his voice.

So, there are at least three of them which were too many for him to confront. He slowly made his way back through the room and out of the rear door.

"What happened?" Amy asked.

"They are lying in wait for us, so we have to get away from here."

"Who are they?" Amy asked, her voice rising.

"Please keep it down or they might hear you. I don't know who they are, but you will be disappointed to know that Mark is one of them."

"Mark?" Amy said with a shocked look on her face. "But he has been the most active against our nemesis. He has always been going here and there, trying new internet cafés, doing everything to defeat whatever it is that is destroying our lives."

"He did this on his own?" Mike asked.

"Yes, he said he did not want to compromise anyone else."

More alarm bells rang in his head. "Maybe we should discuss this somewhere safe," he said, gently holding her arm and guiding her back towards the bicycles.

"Where shall we go?" Amy asked, as we collected the bicycles from where we had hidden them.

"Firstly, let us get away from this place, in case some others turn up and they see us," he said, mounting the bicycle.

Amy mounted her bike and they rode quickly away from the business park, keeping to side roads.

After about 20 minutes, they stopped.

"Where can we go?" Amy asked. "My credit cards were all cancelled in a similar fashion to Greta's and I don't have much money."

"Well, you're not the only one to have a little hideaway. I have an isolated cottage where I go to have a break from modern life. It is too far away to cycle, but I have some cash on me, so if you are willing, we can sneak into the coach station and get a coach there." Mike said with a smile.

"Surely the 'thing' will know about this hideaway, if it registered in your name?" Amy asked.

"Luckily, it is not registered in my name."

"So, whose name is it registered under, a girlfriend?" Amy asked quietly.

God! He thought. *We've just met and yet she sounds jealous.*

"No, it is not a girlfriend. I don't have a girlfriend at the moment. It is not important whose name it is registered under as long as it is not mine, OK!" He answered, a bit sharply.

"Sorry I asked," Amy replied pouting.

"So, are you willing to go to this place?"

"Yes of course, and by the way, it is no interest to me whether you have a girlfriend or not. It is just that I did not want to impose if the place belonged to a girlfriend, OK!" she said, echoing my sharpness of tone.

Oops, he thought.

With that, they mounted the bikes and rode in silence along back roads towards the main coach station.

They dumped the bikes in a lane about a quarter of a mile from the coach station, much to Amy's chagrin. He then gave her enough money for the coach ticket together with information on which coach service to use. They then separated and took different routes into the coach station. He again used the 'stone in the shoe' to disguise his walk. As Amy was experienced at avoiding recognition so he assumed she did something similar.

They sat apart during the coach journey as most coaches have cameras which, for all they knew, may be infiltrated remotely. As agreed earlier, he got off the coach one stop before our true destination. Amy got off at the correct stop and waited until he arrived there on foot.

They then walked to the cottage which he owned under a different name and identity from a different life he experienced several years ago.

He got the door key from his hiding place and they entered the cottage. He had not been there over the months he had been chasing the internet interloper, so the place looked and smelt unlived in.

"You can see that this is a man's place," Amy said with a smile as she looked around the living room.

"Can I open the windows before I suffocate?" She added with a laugh.

She threw open the windows and immediately started tidying the room.

He thought I will never be able to find anything again. But he kept quiet.

"Do you have any food?" Amy asked.

"Not anything you would want to eat," he replied. "It's been months since I have been here. So, whatever is here, and there is not much, will be inedible."

"So, are we on a slimming diet as well as being hounded?" Amy asked with a smile on her face.

"No, we can buy food at the village store. So, make a list of what you want, and I will get it, and before you ask, I'll pay cash so there is no electronic activity."

"What about clothes? I cannot spend the rest of my life in what I am wearing now," Amy said, looking down at her rumpled clothing.

"Well, I am sorry, but I we are not in the best location to purchase new clothes, so what would you suggest?" He said.

"In that case, we will have to go back to our hideaway and retrieve my own clothes," she replied.

He thought amazement must showed on his face, because she added, "Well, if you won't come, I will go myself."

The words 'pig-headed' sprang to his mind but he decided not to voice it.

Chapter 3

The voice of the Controller from the computer was threatening. "You have failed. We thought you had control of that group of saboteurs. Now you have lost the one you call Amy together with the man you call Mike, who is a danger to us. You are aware we do not accept failure."

Mark blanched at the implied threat. He hurriedly answered, "We are on their trail. The bikes they rode had GPS location devices fitted. We know where they are. We are close to recapturing them."

The response was, "Report back tomorrow, and it better be positive news." With that, the computer shut down.

Mark turned to the other two men in the office. "You heard what's wanted. Find those two bastards and quickly if you want to survive."

The men looked at each other with fear in their eyes. "Why are we taking the blame?" One of them asked. "It was you who left them alone with this 'Mike' character," he added.

"Idiot!" Mark shouted. "We are all in trouble. But be sure you will get your comeuppance before me. Now get going to where those bikes are now located and don't fail."

"Shall we bring them back to this office or take them back the hideaway?" One of the men asked.

"Take them to the hideaway. I don't want them knowing I have this office. Now get going," Mark answered, gesturing for them to leave.

"I will kill that bastard Mike when I get him," Mark said to himself. "Things were going smoothly. I had the others in the palm of my hand. They were neutralised until he turned up. God, I hate him."

Muttering to himself he turned away from the computer, left the office, jumped in his car and drove to the original hideaway.

He entered the building and went to what was once Amy's bedroom. The three bodies of his previous colleagues lay on the floor. They had put up a bit of a fight, but the Tasers had quickly neutralised them. He remembered with some delight the look on their faces as he and his two men had walked into the hideaway. Greta looked pleased to see him until the Taser charge hit her. Joe had charged at them and it took three hits from the Tasers to bring him down. Phil looked stunned and was soon actually stunned when the Taser charge hit him. Mark laughed to himself at his own humour.

Now the problem was what to do with them. He had given them an injection which kept them unconscious. But they could not be kept here indefinitely. He had been told to dispense with them, easier said than done. Where can you get rid of three bodies without a comeback? But unless he did something, he knew he would be joining them.

His mind switched to Amy and Mike and although disposing of even more bodies would be a bigger problem, he still looked forward to them being brought here. He would enjoy making them suffer.

Chapter 4

"OK." Mike said. "We will go back for your clothes, but not immediately. I am sure there are a few basic female necessities at the Village Shop. So, let us go there and get food and 'whatever'. Then we can plan how to safely return to the hideaway,"

"Also, it is now my turn." He added with a smile, as he pushed a motorcycle helmet into her hands.

"What's this?" Amy asked. "I have only been on the back of a motorcycle once. I am not sure I am up to it," she added, with her arms outstretched staring at the helmet.

"I think it was you who said, 'You never forget how to ride a bike'," he said, as he gently pushed her towards the door.

They rode into the village. He gave Amy some cash and asked her to enter the village shop alone as he did not want any visible connection between them in case one of them was spotted by CCTV. After 30 minutes or so, she came back to where he had parked the motorbike.

"They are very nosy in that shop. They wanted to know where I was staying, what my name was. Why did I need the items I chose? Did I not bring them from my home? They don't need their security cameras as they end up knowing everything about their customers whether the customer wants it or not."

"So, what did you tell them?" He asked hesitantly.

"Not a lot. I surprised myself. I never thought I was any good at lying, but a fictitious story just flowed from my lips."

"Good," he said. "But what did you tell them?"

"I noticed a caravan park while we were riding here. It's about two miles from the village. I told them I had just arrived and found to my horror that I had left a bag at home in London, hence my need of certain items. By the way, my name is now Jane and I lecture in English at a college in London, OK?"

"Sounds good," he said. "Now I better make my way to the shop and get the food before some local spots us and the gossip starts."

He got food and we returned to his cottage. Amy cooked a meal which they ate, washed down with a bottle of red wine. She retired to the one bedroom and he slept on the sofa in the living room.

Next morning, bright and early, Amy was out of bed, showered and singing in the kitchen.

He thought, *I could get used to this.*

"Come on lazy bones," she shouted from the kitchen. "Get showered. Breakfast is almost ready."

He thought, *I am not sure if I could get used to this.*

After breakfast, Amy asked, "When and how are we going back to hideaway?"

"How is easy; the motorbike. 'When' requires some thought," he answered.

"I would like to go tonight," Amy said.

"Why, what is so urgent?" he asked.

"My friends are maybe dead. I worry Mark may do something to cover-up his crime and destroy the place," Amy said sadly.

"OK. Tonight, it is. Let us consider how we are going to approach the building. By the way, you will find motorbike leathers in that cupboard," he said, pointing to a cupboard under the stairs.

Amy retrieved them, held them against herself noting that they would fit and that they looked feminine. "Whose are they?" Amy asked. "Some previous past love?" she asked with a wicked grin on her face.

"Well, that is in the past," he answered a bit too hastily.

"Oh! Have I touched a nerve?" she asked, grinning widely.

"If it's history you want, let's start with you," he said pointedly. "What is an attractive woman doing without a partner? Or have I touched a nerve?"

"OK. Point taken, let bygones be bygones," Amy answered.

He felt I had been a little bit too brusque as the smile had left her face.

"I am sure the time will come when we open up to one another, but we have serious business ahead and I think we should concentrate on planning our raid," He said, hoping to lessen the tension. She nodded, turned away and went back to examining the motorbike leathers.

So much for my softer approach, he thought.

They decided to approach the building in the evening before it was too dark so they could check for activity. They set off mid-afternoon and rode towards the hideaway making sure they did not break any speeding laws which might bring them to police attention, and which could expose them electronically.

They left the motorbike with their helmets in the panniers a few hundred yards from the building and approach it on foot following the same route they had used on the previous occasion.

They crept up to the back of the building as they had done before. Amy immediately went to her own bedroom window. She gasped out loud and covered her mouth with her hand. She then waved for Mike to come to her side.

He looked through the window and could see the bodies of Amy's friends lying on the floor. They were not moving and looked dead. He put his arms around Amy as the tears rolled down her face. They ducked their heads below the window as they saw the door from the main area into Amy's room start to open. Mike then slowly raised his head such that he could just see over the windowsill. Mark was standing in the room with his back to the window. He was looking down at the bodies and prodding one with his foot. The body moved slightly. Mike whispered to Amy, "Maybe they are alive."

"We have to rescue them," Amy said.

"Yes, but we must find out how many are guarding them, otherwise we could find ourselves on the floor beside them. So please wait here while I go around to the front see if I can check up on them." With that, he slowly made his way around the building to the front. He slowly crept along the front until he was under one of the main room windows. He slowly raised his head and peered through. There was no one present in the room. He then quietly opened the front door, but not quietly enough as he heard Mark shout from Amy's room. "Is that you, Jeff? Did you get that bastard Mike?" The door opened from Amy's room and Mark walked into a right-hand haymaker. He stumbled back into Amy's room before falling onto the floor. Mike followed him and drove his right foot into Mark's jaw. Mark moaned then went quiet. Mike looked up to see Amy staring through the window, a look of shock on her face. He waved for her to come around the front and come in. He then went across and bent down where Joe, Phil and Freda were lying. They were comatose but were breathing. "Thank goodness," he whispered to himself.

At that moment, Amy entered the room. She saw Mark crawling towards Mike. "Look out!" she screamed.

Mike turned, sprang to his feet and aimed a kick at Mark's head. He did not follow through with the kick as Mark rolled on to his back with his hands over his head screaming, "Don't!"

"Get on your feet and sit on that chair," Mike spat the words at him. Mark obeyed with a terrified look on his face. Mike asked Amy to find some rope, which she did, and they then tied Mark securely to the chair, Mike then gagged and blindfolded him, but not before Mark pleaded that he never meant them any harm. Mike had to restrain Amy from attacking Mark, as she shouted. "That he was the lowest form of human being that is possible to meet."

Turning to her three friends who lay on the floor, she asked Mike. "Are they alive?"

"Yes, but we need help and I think we need to get them to hospital ASAP," he said.

"How can we do that quickly? We don't have transport and we don't know how long an ambulance would take to get here," Amy said with a touch of panic in her voice

Mike answered. "I am sure Mark has not been riding that bicycle since he left us, so there must be a car around here somewhere." With that, he went over to Mark and searched him. "Success!" He shouted as he pulled a set of car keys from Mark's pocket, together with a mobile phone. "I am going to look for the car so please stay here and attend to your friends." Mike left the building and found the car parked close by. It was a large BMW. "It looks as through being a Judas is profitable," he murmured to himself.

He started the car and pulled up close to the main door of the building.

As he entered the door, Amy was struggling to aid Freda across the floor of the room. She had Freda's arm draped over her shoulder as she helped her walk in a stumbling fashion towards the door. He took hold of Freda's other arm and they both got her out of the building and into the back of the car. They returned to Amy's bedroom and lifted Joe off the floor. Mike took him in a fireman's lift and with Amy's help got him into the back of the car alongside Freda. They then got Phil to his feet and between them carried him out to the car. They put him in the front passenger seat.

Amy asked, "What now?"

"I want you to drive to the nearest hospital, which is the General. Don't alert them to your presence. Park the car close to A&E and walk away. Use Mark's phone to inform the hospital that three severely injured people are outside in the car and then throw the phone away. I will be following behind you on the motorbike and will pick you up."

"OK," she said. "But I want the clothes I came for."

"Please hurry up and get them. We don't know how long we have got until the rest of Mark's gang turn up. You will also need a bag to carry the clothes as you will be leaving the car at the hospital," He replied.

Fifteen minutes later, Amy came hurrying out of the building grasping a case in one hand and Mark's phone in the other.

"Mark's gang have just called. They are on their way back here, so we better get going." She strode to the car, threw the bag into the boot, jumped into the driver's seat, started the car and drove off with a wave of her hand. He then left the building, quickly retracing his steps to where he had left the motorbike.

He rode the motorbike to the hospital gates where Amy was waiting.

"Is everything OK?" He asked.

"Yes. I left the car, phoned the hospital then hid out of sight. Staff came out of the hospital and started to carry my friends inside. I then scuttled to the gate to meet you." With that, she put on her helmet and with the case of clothes wedged between them they made their way back to his cottage.

Chapter 5

The voice of the Controller coming from the computer was cold. "I simply asked you to deal with one problem person. Not only did you fail to do that, you also lost the other three troublemakers. I think our reliance on you was ill founded. What should we do with you?"

"It wasn't my fault. They snuck up on me. I was concentrating on finishing off the three we had," Mark answered with fear in his voice.

The Controller responded, "We do not want to hear excuses. We want action. You and your bunch of morons have one last chance. Succeed or you all will regret it. We captured on CCTV the motorbike they used to leave the hospital. The registration plate shows the motorbike is owned by someone called John Williams. He resides at Laurel Cottage in Essex. Find him and persuade him to give up the whereabouts of the two who were riding the motorbike and do it now."

"What about the other three who escaped?" Mark asked nervously.

"They are at a hospital. We will take care of them." With that, the computer screen went blank.

"OK. You heard it, get your butts moving out to Laurel Cottage, wherever that is," Mark said, angrily to his men.

"So, you're not going?" One of the men called Hal, asked, looking pointedly at Mark.

"No. I better stay here in case there are more instructions," Mark answered quietly.

The two men looked at each other and then both turned to Mark. "I think you will have to go because we are not going without you. So, it is either with us or on your own."

"OK. If you don't think you can handle it on your own, I better go along," Mark said sharply.

"It's not that we cannot handle it. It is because we don't trust you to tell your Lord and Master the truth. We don't want to take the blame, with you walking scot-free. So now that is all cleared up, let's get going. Oh, and by the way, what happened to your jaw? Really nasty bruises," Hal said with a grin on his face as he's walking towards the door.

Mark gritted his teeth.

Chapter 6

"Well, we got away with it," Mike said.

"Yes, but poor old Freda, Joe and Phil did not. I wonder how they are getting on," Amy replied sorrowfully.

"Unfortunately, there is nothing we can do. We cannot visit and I can guarantee they won't give you updates over the phone. They are in a place where they will be looked after and hopefully, they are safe from Mark," he replied. It did not make her happy but at least she accepted the reasoning.

With that, the lights went out. He tried the phone and got an engaged tone. Alarm bells rang in his head. "I think they have found us," he said, as he looked out of the window into the night.

"How could they have done that?" Amy said, rather shakily. "I thought you said everything here is under another name."

"It is, but somehow they have traced me. It can only be due to this last trip we made. Thinking about it, it could only have been the motorbike. They could have seen the registration plate and traced it to this address. But they cannot know that it is me. They must be checking out the owner. We have to get out of here before they get the connection."

"Where can we go?" Amy asked with a look of concern on her face.

"I wish I knew. I thought this was our hideaway," he replied.

"Hideaway," Amy repeated his word slowly. "I know," Amy said, with a smile on her face. "We can go back to our headquarters, our old hideaway. I bet Mark doesn't live there and they certainly won't expect us to return."

He looked at her. "What a brilliant idea. Let's grab what we can from here and get going."

With some difficulty, they packed clothes etc. into the bag, mounted the motorbike and rode off. He took the opposite direction to that which they wanted to go on the basis if anyone was watching then it might throw them off the scent.

Chapter 7

A car screeched to a halt outside Mike's cottage. Mark and the two men ran up to the front door and not bothering to try the handle, kicked the door in. They rushed into the living room. Finding it empty, they assumed that the occupants were in bed, they then rushed up the stairs to find the bedrooms empty.

"Turn the light on," Mark said sharply to one of the men.

The light switch clicked but no light came on. "Try the phone!" Mark shouted at the man.

"OK, OK, don't lose your head. It is dead," the man replied, putting the phone down.

"Maybe they didn't pay their bill," one of the men said, laughing.

"This is no laughing matter you idiot!" Mark screamed at the man. "Go and check if the motorbike is here."

Once outside, one of the men said to the other, "I have had enough of him."

"So, have I," the other man replied. "Let's get out of here." They quickly got in the car and drove off.

"What is that noise?" Mark asked himself, moving to the door.

"The bastards have deserted me. They will pay for that. They probably think I am the only one being tracked; well, they are now going to find out the error of their ways."

With that, he opened his laptop and typed in a code.

"Yes, have you found the people I asked you to?" The Controller asked in its mechanical voice.

"No, not yet. I have a problem."

"You always seem to be having problems." The Controller replied. "What is it this time?" The tone of the Controller's voice sent a shiver down Mark's spine.

"The men working with me have left. They don't work for you anymore," Mark said quietly.

"You never fail to amaze me as to how many ways you can fail. What are we to do with you? We have promised you riches beyond your dreams and yet you cannot rise to the occasion. We are losing patience with you." The Controller said darkly.

"Just a minute," Mark interjected. "You must have switched off the power and phone to the cottage before we got there and alerted them. So, if any blame is attached, it is yours not mine."

"You must have been too slow getting there. Find them and report back." With that, the screen went dead.

They don't like it when the boot is on the other foot, Mark thought to himself. *Maybe I have been too meek with them.*

His mind went back to the period before the Controller first approached him. Although, at that point in time, he was unaware of the existence of the Controller it had done to him what it had done to the others of the group. His cards were cancelled, his utility bills were not paid, and he lost his job in appalling circumstances.

It then made contact when he was using an internet café. It took over his screen and made him an offer. Money and references you would kill for. He was in a parlous state, so he jumped at the chance to get back into society. The fact that following this path had led him to almost murder his colleagues caused him no concern. He knew his creed of "Every man for himself" had singled him out to the Controller.

The first project they gave him was to hunt for a group of people who had fallen foul of the Controller and been punished but were continuing to probe its system. It took a while, but he found the group and slowly but surely taken them over. He then, by various means, limited their access to computers and diverted them away from other avenues which could have troubled the Controller.

Things had been going well for him. He was building up a nice bank balance, thanks to the money from the Controller. Then Mike had shown up and would undoubtedly spot what was going on and expose the charade.

He was going to enjoy dealing with that bastard Mike and that bitch Amy, but he had to find them first. *Where to look?* that was the problem, then a thought struck him, *The motorbike*! The Controller should be able to track it as it knows the registration number. With that, he powered up his laptop.

"Yes, we are obviously aware that we know the motorbike registration number. We have been monitoring its journey," the Controller said coldly.

"So where is it?" Mark responded quickly. His confidence is his new manner of dealing with the Controller was apparent.

"Why should we tell you of all people? You are stranded without a car. You have failed us numerous times. What good could you do?" The Controller said slowly and deliberately.

Mark's previously felt confidence started to evaporate.

"I know them. I know how they think," Mark replied, his voice bordering on pleading.

"Against our better judgement we will give you one final chance to redeem yourself. I think you know what will happen if you fail. We are sending to your computer a programme allowing you to track the motorbike also the CCTV record of its progress since it left your location." With that, the screen went blank.

Mark thought to himself, *How did I get into this mess?* However, his character did not allow him to accept the truth that it was simply greed. His mindset convinced himself that it was because he was brave and more focused than most.

His confidence somewhat repaired. He phoned for a taxi to take him to a car-hire company.

As he travelled in the taxi, he saw the results of a road accident. There were ambulances and an upside-down car which had obviously burnt out. It was with a smile that he recognised that it was the car which had been driven away by his treacherous helpers. "They had it coming," he quietly whispered to himself. He continued his journey in a happier frame of mind as he convinced himself that he had orchestrated their demise.

Chapter 8

"Are we going directly to the hideout?" Amy shouted in Mike's ear, above the noise of the motorbike.

Mike slowed the motorbike down and came to halt in a lay-by. "I am not sure," he said, as he unbuckled his helmet. "I am concerned. I know we have been careful and followed secondary roads, but I wonder if we are being tracked. What I want to do is find another motorbike and swop its registration plates for ours."

"What!" Amy exclaimed, with a shocked look on her face. "You could be putting some innocent person at risk."

"Well, I am open to suggestions," Mike said with a grin on his face.

"Why don't we dump the motorbike, get a taxi or even two taxis to within a long walking distance of the hideaway, and take a circuitous route to walk there and use the electric bicycles to get around," Amy said, with a smile on her face.

"Hmm. What if we have to get away quickly from the hideaway?" Mike replied.

"OK, we steal a van. We put the motorbike in the van. We drop the motorbike off at the hideaway. We then drive the van away and dump it, or even return it, then do the bit with the taxis; how about that?" Amy said with a bigger smile on her face.

"How good are you at stealing vans?" Mike asked.

"Surely it cannot be that difficult," Amy replied. "Teenagers seem to do it all the time."

"Well, we will have to give it a try," Mike said with a little smile. He then started the motorbike up and moved out of the lay-by.

He said that with confidence. I think he has had a chequered life, Amy thought to herself as they drove towards the town.

"Can I ask why we're driving around places that don't seem to have any vans?" Amy asked, shouting into Mike's ear.

Mike slowed the bike down and shouted back, "Stealing a van is one thing, but lifting the motorbike into the van is another. I am looking for places to get our hands-on planks or similar material that we can use as a ramp to allow us to ride the bike into the van. Then when we get the van, you can drive it back to the location of the planks while I follow on the bike. We can then hopefully get the bike into the van without attracting too much attention."

As they sat in the hideaway, Amy thought to herself that she was surprised how easily it had all gone including Mike returning the van and making his way back to the hideaway by taxi and on foot. She also smiled when she visualised the look on the van owner's face when he found three planks of wood in his van.

"So, what's our plan?" Amy asked.

"The first thing I want to do is revisit the business park that was given the all-clear by Mark. At the moment it is our only lead to the Evil One," Mike replied.

"The what?" Asked Amy, with a look of surprise on her face.

"Well, I don't like the name Controller. It implies we are controlled, and we are not. So, as we must call it something, so I thought of the Evil One. Got any better ideas?" Mike replied with a smile on his face.

"My cat could have thought of a better name than the Evil One," Amy said, with a laugh.

"OK how about you and your cat come up with a name," Mike said, struggling to stop chuckling.

"How about Infiltrator?" Amy suggested.

"That's worse than mine," Mike said, his eyes crying with laughter.

"I suppose you want Evil Infiltrator One," Amy replied, struggling to speak through her laughter.

"OK you win, Infiltrator it is," Mike said, shrugging his shoulders.

"Good. I knew my name was the best one. So when do we start?" Amy asked.

"It will have to be at night, and it is too late tonight, so we start tomorrow," Mike replied. "So, let us get some shut-eye."

As Amy was closing the door of her bedroom, Mike said, "Yours wasn't the best name, it was just I could not put up with any more of your moaning." He just managed to shut the door of his room before one of Amy's shoes clattered against it. Amy smiled to herself as she went into her room thinking I do not know what the outcome of this combined venture is going to be. But I do know it is going to be fun.

Chapter 9

"Where the hell are they going?" Mark asked himself as he followed the route of the motorbike shown on his computer. "They seem to be going around in circles then the motorbike goes into a dead zone where there are no cameras and never comes out; which is strange as I have driven through that zone and did not see it. I wonder if I missed it?"

Quickly turning his car around, he drove back into the zone where the motorbike disappeared. There was no motorbike to be seen and as he sat there pondering and examining the CCTV recording of the area leading into the zone, he noticed they showed a van entering the zone. Something clicked in his mind as he thought he had seen that van elsewhere on the CCTV recordings.

He quickly scanned back through the recordings on the computer and said to himself, "Yes," as he saw the image of the van parked in a street about a mile from where he was sat. He also noticed on the recording that the motorbike slowed down as it passed the van.

Is there any connection? he wondered.

He again quickly turned his car around and headed to the street where the van had been previously parked; it was there. He got out of the car and walked around the van inspecting it. Suddenly a huge man was beside him. "Thinking of taking it again?" he asked in a threatening manner, his face only inches away from Mark's face.

"No. No," Mark replied as he staggered back in shock. "I am trying to find the person who took it."

"Why?" Asked the man as he approached Mark again. "They used the van to steal something of mine," Mark spluttered, his mind working overtime on how to calm the threat from the man.

"What did they steal?" The man asked still in a threatening manner.

"A motorbike," Mark answered his voice little more than a squeak.

The man stepped back. "That will explain why three planks of wood were left in the van. They must have used them to load the bike."

"Well, your motorbike isn't here so I suggest you 'push off'." The man added as he walked away from the van.

Mark got back into his car. "I've got them!" He shouted. I just need to inform the Controller about the van registration number then we will know where they are hiding." He hastily typed a note on his computer and included the registration number. Within ten minutes, a record of the van's movements appeared on his computer. He scrolled through the images and could not believe his eyes when he saw the old hideout.

"They think they're clever, but I am better than them. They are in for a shock when we get them," he said out loud to himself. It was when he said 'we' that it clicked there was no 'we' and he realised that he was alone. His two helpers who had acted as muscle were now dead. Should he ask the Controller for help? He shuddered at the thought of what the voice may do. No. He was on his own. His confidence started to rise as he considered what he was going to do with Mike and Amy. Now he must plan his attack and this time he would be armed. He returned to his covert office and collected the shotgun.

Chapter 10

When Mike awoke in the morning, he could smell that breakfast was underway. Easing himself into the main room he could see Amy in the small kitchen quietly humming a tune as she turned bacon over in the frying pan.

"What a wonderful smell to wake up to." He said as he moved across room towards her.

"Oh, you're up. Good, you can set the table. Cutlery is in that draw." She said pointing to a small set of drawers.

Settling down, they had breakfast almost in silence. After clearing the dishes, Amy asked, "What are our plans for today?"

"First thing we have to do is to make this place secure. Everyman and his dog have keys and access to it."

"I would like to find out what has happened to Greta, Bill and Joe," Amy said, with a determined look on her face.

"I think that's a mistake," Mike said. "But if you feel so strongly about it then you must find out, but you will have to do it on your own."

"OK I will," Amy answered in a sharp voice.

"It is not that I don't think about them but I feel we have little time to protect ourselves so we have to share the jobs which must be done," Mike said gently, putting his hand on Amy's arm.

"I know you're right," Amy said, putting her hand over his. "But I feel as if I betrayed them."

"You did not betray them," Mike interrupted. "You and I were just lucky to be away from here, otherwise we both could be in the hospital with your friends."

"Yes, you are right again, which is getting a bit wearing," she said with a hint of a smile on her face.

Mike smiled to himself, glad that the old Amy was showing through.

Heavily disguised, Amy left to walk to the nearest bus stop,

Mike examined the building making a list of items needed to improve their protection. He then, also disguised, walked for a mile before hailing a taxi.

As Amy approached the hospital, she wondered on the best method to see her friends without giving herself away to the Infiltrator. Approaching the front desk seemed risky unless she could carry-off giving a false name, which she doubted. Another method of entry could be to assume a profession which would gain unrestricted access to the wards. Thinking about who had unrestricted access to wards other than medical staff, she realised that there was another group. 'Cleaners'. *I wonder where they keep their equipment*, she whispered to herself. *I am sure it won't be in the front of the building, so let's try the back.* With these thoughts, she set off to reconnoitre the back of the hospital. After 15 to 20 minutes, which felt much longer as she worked on being inconspicuous, she saw someone approaching the door at the rear of the hospital. Amy quickly caught up with her and in a flustered voice said this was her first day and that she was 'gutted' that it looked like she was going to be late. The other person smiled, used the code to open the door and they both entered. "Where do you have to go?" the person asked.

"I have to check in with the Cleaning Supervisor," Amy answered, hoping that the person was not the Cleaning Supervisor.

"Well, it is not too far. If you go along that corridor you will come to her office." With that, the person turned and walked off in the opposite direction.

"Whew. That was a bit of luck!" Amy said quietly.

She slowly walked along the corridor looking into the rooms which were leading off it. After a few false starts, she came to one which looked like the storage room for clothes destined for the laundry. She quickly moved inside and closed the door behind her. She started rummaging through the clothes hoping to find one that looked like a cleaner's overall. Suddenly, the door to the corridor opened and a man walked in. He looked surprised to see her.

"Can I help you?" He asked in a puzzled manner.

"Oh," Amy said, with her sweetest smile on her face. "You have caught me. I am a cleaner and have just started, and I forgot my Overall. I was hoping to find one I could use and save myself some trouble."

"Yes, that Jill can be a bit of a monster," he said. "Don't use a dirty one, we have plenty of laundered ones through here." With that, he guided her through to another room which had racks of clean clothes.

"Help yourself," he said, then walked through another doorway closing the door behind him.

"This is really my lucky day," Amy said, her face beaming. Moving along the racks of clothes she carefully chose a cleaner's overall. She put it on after carefully hiding her own garments behind the clothes racks.

She left the room and walked away from the direction of the Cleaner Supervisors office not wanting to be found out as an imposter.

Mike gradually found and purchased the items he had listed. Whilst not large items there were too many to carry so he took a taxi back to the hideout. Leaving the taxi, he expected to find the building deserted, but as he approached the building, he thought he saw a slight movement through the window. He could not believe that Amy was back already, so who was it?

Leaving the items, he had purchased on the ground, he carefully approached the door of the hideaway. Suddenly it was flung open and Mark stood there with a shotgun which was pointed at Mike's head.

"So big shot. You're not so clever now?" Mark said, gesturing with the gun for Mike to enter the building.

"Where's that stupid bitch Amy?" Mark asked his face twisted in hate.

"She has had enough of this nonsense and she has left the country," Mike lied.

"Pity, I had big ideas for her. Now, it will be just you." Mark said as he pushed the shotgun barrel into Mike's stomach.

Mike quickly pushed the barrel of the gun to one side with one hand and punched Mark in the throat with the other hand. As one of Mark's hands went automatically up to his damaged throat Mike pulled the gun away from him. The gun went-off harmlessly and Mark screamed as his finger almost broke as the gun was wrenched from his grasp. Mike kicked Mark's legs from under him.

Crouching on the floor, Mark looked at Mike with terror in his eyes. "Don't kill me. I can help you get the Controller."

"And how will you do that?" Mike asked.

"I know where his ground station is and I can show you," Mark said, as he tried to get to his feet.

Mike pushed him back onto the floor and said, "It wouldn't be the Eastleigh Business Park by any chance?"

Mark looked shocked. "You may know where it is, but it is not easy to get into and it can be dangerous. I know how to get in safely," he added.

"Why should we trust you? You were ready to kill your friends to benefit yourself," Mike said viciously.

Ha, he said. *'We' and not 'me' so Amy is still involved, I can probably still get them both if I play this right,* Mark thought to himself.

"I have found out that you cannot trust the Controller. I want to break away from it, but I cannot do it on my own. I need help," Mark said in pleading voice.

I don't believe him, nor do I trust him but maybe I can use him to get closer to the Infiltrator? Mike thought.

"OK, maybe we can work together to finish this nuisance once and for all," Mike said as he pulled Mark to his feet. "But be sure I will use this gun on you if you try to double-cross me." He added with venom.

Chapter 11

Amy made her way to the reception area. She had to find a plan of the hospital otherwise she could be wandering around aimlessly.

She got some strange looks from the reception staff as they watched her scan the plan.

Smiling at them and touching her head as if she had forgotten something seemed to ease the looks, she was getting.

She scurried down a corridor which led to the lifts, aiming to start on the Accident and Emergency wards first.

She quickly looked at the people lying in the beds in the four wards. Finally, a Ward Sister stopped her and asked her what she was doing. Amy quickly thought and said, "I was here a few days ago and saw three people who had been left in the car park. They looked so ill and forlorn. I was just wondering what had happened to them."

The sister's face changed and hardened. "What do you know about those people?" She asked firmly.

"Well, nothing other than I felt sorry for them," Amy replied as she tried to distance herself from the sister.

"Well, I suggest you mind your own business and get back to your work." With that, the sister turned and walked away.

How strange, Amy thought as she slowly moved away from the A&E section.

She suddenly felt a hand on her arm. She turned quickly; her heart pumping with shock. A young nurse stood there.

"I couldn't help hearing that you were enquiring about those three poor people. I know the sister is following advice from the hospital management and not saying anything, but I think people should know." With that, she beckoned Amy into a side room.

"The three people who were found outside the hospital had been drugged but were essentially O.K. They were wired up and put on an intravenous drip to clear the drugs. Sometime later people were complaining that the computer systems were going haywire."

At this juncture, Amy's mental antenna twitched at the mention of computers.

The nurse continued, "Everyone was so busy checking the main computer screens that it was 30 minutes or so before they thought to check the actual medical equipment. It was then they found that the quantity of intravenous drugs to the three people you are enquiring about had been increased enormously and all warning signals had been switched off."

"So, what happened to the three people?" Amy asked, her heart sinking as she spoke.

"They didn't make it. The hospital is keeping quiet about the problem as they search for those responsible."

"Tell them to stop searching. I know it's a 'what' not a 'who' that is responsible, and they will never find it." With that, Amy spun on her heel and with tears welling from her eyes, walked away as quickly as possible towards the lifts to get back to the room which held her clothes.

Chapter 12

"So how do you contact what you call the Controller?" Mike asked.

"I speak to it through a phone," Mark said quietly.

"What number do you use?"

"I don't dial a number; the phone is permanently connected."

"Let me see it," Mike said holding out his hand.

"I want it back," Mark said huffily as he handed the phone over to Mike.

Mike looked at the phone, gave it some thought and then said to Mark, "I want you to contact them and tell them that you have eliminated both of us. Give them any story you like but make it believable." Mike then handed the phone back to Mark. "Do it now and put it on speaker mode. I want to hear what is said," he ordered, pointing the shotgun directly at Mark.

Mark took the phone and clicked it on.

"Yes, what do you want now?" the Controller said. "I hope you have some positive news for your sake."

"I have," Mark replied. "I have eliminated both of those troublemakers you sent me after."

"How?" asked the Controller.

"I shot them."

"Where are the bodies?" asked the Controller.

"Where do you think? I buried them," Mark answered scornfully.

"So, you are the only one left from that troublesome crowd?" The Controller said quietly.

Before Mark could answer, Mike pulled the phone out of Mark's hand and threw it out of the open door then slammed the door shut. The phone exploded and pieces of it slammed into the door.

Mark's face went white, his eyes wide and staring. "My God, it tried to kill me after all I have done for it."

"Maybe it is all you deserve," Mike remarked pointedly. "You were happy to see others die."

"I wasn't happy, it was either them or me. You would have done the same."

"Don't ever compare me to yourself, you worthless piece of shit." In his fury, Mike thrust the gun up under Mark's chin. Mark screamed and staggered backwards.

The door opened and Amy entered the room.

"What is he doing here?" She asked, staring at Mark.

"I am beginning to wonder myself," Mike replied. "But I think we are stuck with him until he leads us to the Infiltrator."

Mark realising, he was not going to be shot dead, regained some composure and piped in. "Who and what is the Infiltrator?"

"It is what you call the Controller," Mike replied. "Now shut up and sit in that chair. Amy and I have to talk."

Mike and Amy moved to the far end of the room away from Mark with Mike positioning himself so that he could keep an eye on Mark. He and Amy then began talking in low voices. Mark could not make out the words being said but could hear that Amy was sobbing.

Mark thought to himself, *They think they have the better of me, but I will show them. I will take them to where the Controller is possibly located, if only to get my revenge. But then it will be my turn and they will pay for this harassment.*

"Did you manage to get into the hospital?" Mike asked.

Amy started sobbing. "Yes, I got in. It was horrible. The Infiltrator had found them then interfered with the computers and the equipment and poisoned my friends. They are dead and that bastard over there is as guilty as anyone." She spat the words out pointing at Mark, "How can you deal with him, he is evil."

"He is our guide to the Infiltrator. Once we know where it is, we will dispense with him one way or another. That I promise you."

"What are they talking about?" Mark asked himself. "She pointed at me and her look was venomous. So what! The boot will be on the other foot shortly," he smiled to himself.

"OK. Let's start planning. Can we take Mark's car?" Amy asked.

I am not sure it looks as though he has lost his protected status so the car may be targeted," Mike said.

"No, it should be OK. I used a false name to hire the car," Mark interrupted.

"Good, so we use the car. Do we go now during daytime or do we wait for night?" Amy asked Mike.

Mark again interrupted, "Night would be best, there will be less people there."

"Night it is. So, let us rest up and we will move on them tonight," Mike said, moving towards a chair.

Amy stood rigidly during these exchanges, her eyes staring at Mark with undisguised hatred.

"I am going into my own room. I cannot stand being in the same room as him," she said, gesturing towards Mark as she left.

Wait until it is my turn. She won't know what hit her, Mark thought, his face twisted with hate.

He quickly composed himself as he saw Mike was staring at him.

"Just say when you're ready," he said to Mike, with a weak grin on his face.

Mike turned away in disgust.

"He will get what's coming to him as well," Mark muttered to himself.

As dusk settled, Mike gathered Amy and Mark together. "We don't really know what we will meet or what will happen. So be careful, no heroics. Now into the car. Mark, you are driving."

How do I get those two? Mark thought to himself as he positioned himself in the driving seat. "Do I wait until we are in the building or do I cause a commotion as we are driving in and alert the Controller's helpers?"

The question was answered for him as Mike, who was in the front passenger seat, put the shotgun across his knees and said, "If you so much as look as if you will betray us, I will open up your guts with this shotgun."

Mark gulped and started the car. *God, I hate him*, he thought. *Somehow, sometime, I will get him. But I think I will have to wait until I somehow get help from the Controller's men.*

Mike thought as he glanced at the vicious look on Mark's face. *Have I made the correct decision letting him help us? I don't trust him, and I will certainly have to keep an eye on him.*

Mark slowed the car as they approached the business park.

"Stop here," Mike said, just outside the entrance to the complex.

"I can go further in," Mark said.

"I said stop here, and give me the car keys," Mike hissed angrily.

The car stopped. "We go in on foot, and no funny business," Mike said looking directly at Mark.

Just wait. My time will come, thought Mark as he handed the car keys over.

As they approached the building pointed out by Mark, they could see lights and movement through the windows.

They quietly approached the door at the front of the building. It was locked. As they moved around to the back, Mike saw that the windows were curtained such that any lights inside would show up at night, but no one could see into the building.

The back door was also locked so they moved further around the building to what looked like a loading bay. Here they had some luck as the shutter door had not been lowered fully and was not engaged. Both Mike and Mark got their hands under the bottom of the door and slowly started to lift it. It made a screeching noise as it lifted and both stood back waiting for the occupants to investigate the noise. After a couple of minutes when no one came, they pushed the shutter open such that they could crawl inside.

Mark got through first. He turned and slammed the shutter door down so that it trapped Mike.

"Not so clever now are you," Mark said. He brought his foot back to kick Mike in the head when he saw the barrel of the shotgun appear under the door. He could also just make out Amy's face. He turned and ran into the main part of the building hoping not to get shot in the back.

As he was face down, Mike arched his back and lifted the shutter such that he could slide back out onto the loading bay. Amy had scrambled to her own feet and looked wide-eyed at Mike.

"Another few seconds and I might have killed him," she said, as tears flowed down her cheeks. Mike took her in his arms and hugged her closely.

"You probably saved my life or at least serious injury and that bastard would have deserved everything that you did to him." His words did not seem to console her as her body shook and she sobbed deeply into his shoulder as he held her tighter.

"Before these last few days I had never even hit anyone, and here I am almost ready to kill a person. What is happening to me?" she wailed.

Mike had no answer, so he just hugged her until her sobbing got less.

"We have to do something," Mike said. "God knows what he's up to inside that building. We could have a horde descend upon us. If you wish you can go back to the car and I will follow him in."

"No, I am here to help. I just had a shock which I will get over. Tell me what you want me to do to get that bastard." The fury in Amy's voice belied her previous anguish.

Wow. She has got some spirit, Mike thought, smiling to himself.

"Firstly, we have to get through that door. I am sorry but when I lift it you have to cover me with the shotgun as we don't know what is waiting for us on the other side."

Amy gulped but took the shotgun back from Mike. "OK let's do it," she said.

Mike slowly raised the shutter nervously realising how exposed he was to any attack from inside the room. As soon as the lifted door made a suitable gap with the floor, Amy crouched down with the shotgun at the ready.

The room was empty. Unsure whether to feel glad or disappointed they both crept inside. Mike continued holding the door open until Amy moved an empty bin and positioned it such that it stopped the door sliding shut.

Mike took the shotgun off Amy and started to move towards the door leading into the interior of the building.

"Wait," Amy said, getting hold of Mike's arm. "Why have we not heard any noise from the people in there or even from Mark? There is something strange going on. Please let us proceed carefully."

Taking Amy's warning seriously, Mike slowly opened the door and thrust the gun through the opening ready to fire at anyone lurking there.

The room was empty except for a piece of equipment positioned in the centre.

A fluctuation light beam emanated from it. The illusion of people moving inside the room which he had seen at the window earlier must have been created by this light.

"Where's Mark?" Amy whispered.

"There must be another door somewhere," Mike replied,

"What is that over there?" Amy said, pointing to a corner of the room.

"It's a trapdoor in the floor. There must be a cellar," Mike said as he quietly moved toward it.

As he opened the trapdoor, Mike could hear an electrical hum and could see lights. The trapdoor hinges let out a screech as he opened it further. Suddenly the lights he had seen in the cellar went out.

"Well. there is definitely someone down there," remarked Mike, as he looked at Amy.

"Please be careful," Amy said. "Close the door and let us think about what to do. I think Mark will be desperate and dangerous."

As she said that, a length of metal piping was suddenly thrust up out the cellar narrowly missing Mike's throat. Mike let go of the door which slammed closed catching the pipe and pivoting it on the edge of the trapdoor opening. A yelp came from below as the pipe was snatched from the perpetrator's hand by the weight of the door.

Mike grabbed the pipe and pulled it into the room. The door closed fully.

"Look," Amy said pointing to a significant splash of blood on the end of the pipe.

"I hope that's Mark's blood, he deserved it," she said vehemently.

"You stand here and keep the door closed while I move that piece of equipment onto it," he said to Amy.

Mike tugged and heaved the equipment over the floor until it sat on the door.

"Assuming there is no other exit, we have put Mark out of action," Mike said putting his arms around Amy. He was quietly pleased when she snuggled closer to him.

"Yes, we have, so let us go and have some food and maybe find a bed for the night," Amy said quietly, looking up into Mike's face.

Mike's heart leapt and he hugged her and replied, "That is the best idea I have heard for days. Let's go."

They walked back out to the car and drove to a nearby restaurant.

They decided not to talk about the ongoing problem over the meal but warmly talked about their previous lives. It was clear to any observer how close they were getting to each other, not only physically as they leaned towards each other over the table but affectionately as they stared into each other's eyes as they spoke.

They left the restaurant with arms around each other.

"Now where?" Mike asked as they approached the car.

"Well, there are beds back at the hideaway," Amy replied with a cheeky grin on her face.

They drove back to the hideaway without much conversation, both thinking of the next few hours.

The hideaway was as how they had left it. Mike scooped Amy into his arms as they entered the building and they gently kissed. He carried her into her own bedroom. They quickly struggled out of their clothes and laid on the bed entwined.

Chapter 13

"God, I hate him," Mark muttered to himself as he grasped his cut hand. Stumbling through the darkness he found the light switch. With the light on, he could see the extent of the cut across the palm of his hand. He blanched at the depth of the cut and the amount of blood leaking from it.

"So, you are still alive!" the voice of the Controller came out of the tunnel which extended from one end of the cellar.

Mark jumped at the sound and looked desperately around for a means of escape.

"Do not panic, you can be of use to me," the Controller said.

"How can I trust you? You tried to kill me," Mike replied with more bravado then he felt.

"That was then. Now is now," the Controller said. "And what alternatives do you have available," it added.

"Who, or what are you?" Mark asked fearfully.

"I am your best friend or your worst enemy so keep that in mind," the Controller replied.

Mark slumped to the floor, "I can't take any more. No real friends, a leader I cannot see, no future by the look of it. Just finish me off and get it over with," Mark shouted out tearfully.

There was silence from the Controller after this outburst.

"Well, say something!" Mark shouted.

Silence again.

"Say something," Mark repeated in a whisper, his head bowed.

"You are a pathetic creature, but still of some use. Fulfil the last order I gave you and I will change your life for the better," the Controller said in a cold manner.

"You promised me the same last time and then tried to kill me. Why should I believe you?" Mark shouted, rising to his feet.

"You failed last time and almost paid the price, so now you know it is either you or those other two. So, make your decision," the Controller said.

"You have to help me. They do not trust me, so I can't get close to them," Mark said.

"I will help you, but you have to make them go to a vulnerable place where I can reach them," the Controller replied.

"How do I get out of here?" Mark asked.

"There is a ventilator opening at the far end of this tunnel. Use that. Go to the BT Phone Shop in town, there will be a phone waiting for you there and I will contact you. I will switch off the deterrents until you are clear of the tunnel." With that, the Controller went silent.

Making his way along the tunnel, Mark could see little sign of what constituted the Controller. He eventually came to the ventilation shaft which had a mesh door leading to the outside. It was held closed by a sliding bolt which was easily opened. Within minutes he was outside. He found himself located about 30 metres from the tunnel site building. *Now I must find those two. Where could they be?* Mark pondered. *I know,* he thought. *They will come back here. They are too soft. They would not let me die and for it to be on their conscience. Their stupidity will be the end of them.* He then started walking to the BT Phone Shop. Where, as expected, a phone was waiting for him.

"Plan, plan, after they come back to the tunnel site, I have to be able to follow them when they leave. The bastard Mike took my car, so I need another one."

He took out the phone and started looking for car-hire companies.

Chapter 14

Mike woke up with a start. It took a few seconds before he recalled where he was. Then he felt the bed beside him only to find Amy was not there. Then the smell of bacon cooking wafted to his nostrils. He smiled as he thought to himself, *I think I have landed in heaven.*

The door opened and Amy popped her head into the bedroom. "Come on lazy bones, breakfast is ready."

I am definitely in heaven, Mike again thought as he got out of bed. He scrambled into his clothes and entered the main room of the building. Breakfast was laid out on a table with Amy sitting there with a big smile on her face.

"I think all this work deserves a kiss," Mike said as he moved around the table towards Amy.

"Is that all?" Amy said smiling as she offered her lips up to Mike.

With breakfast and the washing up out of the way, Mike took his shower and sat with Amy at the now empty table.

"What is our next move?" Amy asked.

"I think we have to return to the business site if only to release Mark," Mike said. "I don't like him, nor do I trust him, but we cannot let him starve to death in that cellar," he added.

"Unfortunately, you are right, although it goes against the grain considering all the damage he has done," Amy replied with a grim look on her face.

Not much was said as they drove back to the site. They parked the car close to the building and walked to shutter door with Mike carrying the shotgun.

"It doesn't look like it has been moved since we left," Amy remarked.

"Good, let's get it open." With that, they both got hold of the bottom of the shutter and raised it. Amy went inside and again placed the bin such that it held the shutter open. Mike then entered the room and together they moved the equipment off the trapdoor.

"You stay here, and I will go into the cellar and find Mark," Mike said as he opened the trap door making sure he was not exposed to a possible second pipe being thrust up at him.

"Lights are on but no sign of Mark. He is probably further into the cellar." Mike climbed down the ladder into the cellar hanging onto the ladder with one hand whilst having the shotgun ready in the other hand.

Mike shouted up to Amy, "Still no sign of him here but there seems to be a tunnel leading off this cellar. I will check there."

"Please be careful. I don't want to lose you now!" Amy shouted back.

Mike thought, *That sounds very positive.* His heart warmed to think she was returning his feelings.

"I knew they would turn up here. I am a genius," Mark whispered to himself as he saw their car arrive.

"I can't attack them here. They have the shotgun. Best wait and catch them unaware." Having convinced himself, Mark sat back in his hiding place and waited.

Mike carefully entered the tunnel aiming the shotgun ahead ready to fire at any signs of an attack. Surprised to find that Mark was not in the tunnel, he started examining the tunnel itself. *If this is the headquarter of the Infiltrator, then where is all the equipment?*

As he slowly moved through the tunnel, he saw the ventilation opening. "That's how he escaped. I wonder where the rat is now."

Warning signs flashed in his mind and he hurried back to trapdoor opening. "Amy!" he shouted. "Mark has escaped, he could be anywhere." Thrusting the shotgun up through the trapdoor opening he said, "Take the gun. I don't need it, keep your eyes peeled and don't be afraid to use it if he turns up. I am going to examine this place a little more closely."

Amy hurriedly took hold of the shotgun and nervously scanned the room for any signs of Mark.

Mike was puzzled as to how this cellar and tunnel could be important to the Infiltrator when there was no equipment to be seen. *Maybe I am fixating on equipment I would recognise, there could be other ways of transmitting code etc. which is beyond our knowledge,* Mike thought.

With that in mind, he began examining the cellar walls and floor. He soon realised that the cellar and tunnel were made with a material which at first glance looked like a type of plastic. As he prodded and pushed the walls, it became clear that they stood independent of the surrounding cellar walls if fact forming a room inside a room.

Suddenly, the walls started to glow, and a voice said, "Hello Mike. We meet at last."

Mike did not wait. He raced through the tunnel and scrambled up the ladder. He managed to slam the trapdoor closed just as a flash like a lightning bolt shot across the cellar, its intensity causing the trapdoor to shudder.

Amy stood wide-eyed, "What happened?"

"It's down there," Mike said, trying to get his breath back. "It tried to kill me."

"What can we do about it?" Amy asked.

"I am at a loss. It is not a piece of equipment as we know it. It is built into the walls of the cellar. I would not know where to begin in order to stop it," Mike said.

"How about using water? Electrical equipment does not like water." Amy said.

"Brilliant," Mike said, throwing his arms around Amy. "But it will take a lot of water to fill the cellar and tunnel. So, we need to find a source of a lot of water. Something like a fire hydrant would do."

"I bet there is fire hydrant somewhere on this Business Park. If we can find it then all we will need is a hose," Amy said.

"Yes, you are right again, let's start looking."

"What are they up to?" Mark whispered to himself, as he spotted Mike and Amy leaving the building and walking further into the business park. He noticed they were looking in all directions as they walked.

"Are they looking for me?" he asked himself. Then they halted about ten metres from the building they had left. They talked and pointed at something which looked like a fire hydrant. It became clear to him. They plan to drown the Controller.

I should warn the Controller, thought Mark. *But then again, if those two are successful it would get the Controller off my back. What to do?* he slumped back in the car seat where he had been hiding.

As they walked, Mike thought about what they had found. He turned to Amy, "I cannot believe that our communication systems are being usurped by whatever is in that tunnel. There has to be something else."

"So, what do we do?" Amy asked.

"I think we are struggling, so I suggest we step back from this problem have some food, rest, then consider our options," Mike replied.

They walked back to the building, closed the shutter and moved to the car.

As they drove away, Mark started his new hire car and followed them.

They stopped at a fast food outlet where they chose some take-out food. Mike then drove to the hideaway and parked it a walking distance away from the building.

"I wonder what has become of Mark," Amy said as they settled around the table.

"Why don't you ask me?"

They both spun around to find Mark entering the room.

Mike dived across the room to get hold of the shotgun.

"You don't need that," Mark said with his hands raised above his head.

"I come in peace."

Mike aimed the shotgun at him. "You have two minutes to explain yourself, or by God I will kill you."

"You don't trust me, and I can understand why. But I have changed. What you call the Infiltrator and I call the Controller has betrayed me and I want to see it destroyed."

"This sound like a replay of your last entreaty, you need to do better." Mike said viciously.

Suddenly there was a muffled bang. Mark's jacket seemed to disintegrate, his eyes bulged, his mouth dropped open and blood gushed out. He dropped to the floor lifeless.

Mike and Amy both stared at Mark's body. They were frozen to the spot. Slowly they looked at each other and suddenly realised they were splattered with the remnants of Mark's jacket and what could only be parts of his body.

Amy's face went white and she started swaying.

Mike dropped the shotgun and grabbed hold of her just as she was starting to crumple.

He carried her into her bedroom and laid her on the bed. He sat on the bed, his mind in a whirl. He concluded that the Infiltrator must have been listening to the conversation, it would have heard Mark's betrayal and for the second time taken action against him, probably using another exploding phone.

Suddenly it hit him, the Infiltrator will also now know that we are here. "God, we are on the run again," he said with a grimace.

Amy started to stir and as soon as she sat up she said, "We need to get organised quickly and get out of here. It knows where we are."

Still groggy, she got off the bed, looked down at her clothes and headed towards the shower. Turning to Mike she said, "I don't care if the evil thing is present in this room, I am getting cleaned up before I go anywhere."

Whilst she was in the shower, he gathered what clothes were available which would probably fit him and put them beside the door.

He trotted out to where he had parked the car they had arrived in and drove it back to the hideaway.

Amy was out of the shower and had gathered what she wanted to take with her. Mike showered and changed clothes.

They quickly loaded the stuff in the car including the contaminated clothes they had worn.

"We cannot just leave Mark's body here," Amy said.

"I think we can. His death will look like an accident. We can notify the police about hearing an explosion in the building. We do it from a public phone, therefore we remain anonymous and he will have a decent funeral, but that is all we can do. But I cannot leave the motorbike here as the police will eventually trace its ownership to me so we have to take it with us."

"The first thing we do is get away from this place in case the Infiltrator is sending other people. You take the car and I will take the motorbike then we make the call to the police and head to my house," Mike said.

"But the Infiltrator knows where you live," Amy said.

"I realise that, but if we are to fight this thing, we need more equipment and the easiest way to get it is at my house. We just have to be careful and not let them track us."

They stopped in a lane which they noticed had no cameras, then Mike disguised himself as much as possible, walked to a nearby public phone box and made the 999 call. He ignored all the questions which were thrown at him by the operator and returned to the car.

They both rode and drove in silence, each mulling over in their mind what their future might be. That is if they had a future.

They parked one street away from Mike's home.

"We can approach the back of the house from here. I will scale the fence and let you in."

"If you can climb the fence so can I," Amy replied.

Mike noted the fence offered no problem to Amy and they both approached the backdoor of the house.

"Looks OK," Mike said as he peered through the window. "Everything looks as untidy as I left it."

"I can see the 'real' you is appearing," Amy said with a laugh.

They entered the house. Amy was shocked to see the remnants of the computer screen embedded in the wall.

"You had a close shave," she said, pointing to the wrecked computer.

"Don't remind me. I get a shiver every time I think of it," Mike replied.

While Mike gathered up all the equipment, he asked Amy to scrutinise the street from the upstairs windows.

"It seems 'all clear'!" she shouted to Mike.

"Good. Because we need to bring the car here to carry all this gear. You go and get the car and I will get the motorbike," Mike replied.

After they returned, they packed the equipment into the car.

"Where to now?" Amy asked.

"Where did you live before the problems started?" Mike asked.

"It would be no good going there," Amy answered hurriedly, turning away from Mike.

"I did not say we should go there. Out of interest I only asked where you lived previously," Mike said quietly with a questioning look on his face.

"I prefer not to talk about it if you don't mind?" Amy responded sharply.

"OK, OK, sorry if I have touched a nerve," Mike said, hands in the air as if surrendering.

"You haven't touched a nerve," Amy said, glaring at Mike. But Mike had turned away and getting into the car.

I definitely touched a nerve, Mike thought as he arranged himself in the driving seat of the car.

Amy got into the passenger seat in silence and stared straight ahead out through the windscreen.

As they drove along in silence, Mike thought about Amy's reticence to talk about her early life. He then realised that in the original meeting with the group, Amy had been the only one, other than Mark, not to give any indication of what had forced her to abandon her normal life and become one of the sentinels. *Strange,* he thought.

"Where are we going?" Amy asked quietly.

"We are going to a caravan site I know of. It is not too far out of town and we can stay there incognito."

Amy lapsed back into silence.

"Cat got your tongue?" Mike asked.

"I am sorry for what I said earlier, or should I say for what I did not say. I get a bit upset when I think about how my life changed due to that monster," Amy said, her eyes filling up.

"You don't have to tell me anything that you do not want to," Mike started to say but Amy interrupted.

"I do, you deserve to know after all you have done to help. My story is not a lot different to others. I worked in local government. I was engaged to be married. We lived together in a nice apartment. I then asked too many questions about the leasing of a business building and my life fell apart. I was accused of conniving with Builders to give them preferential bidding rights on land. My fiancé also worked in local government and following the accusation he distanced himself from me, I assume to protect his own job. He left our apartment. My job was taken from me. I have no living close relatives. I was lost. The story was in the local paper so anyone who knew me became aware of the 'so called crime'. You certainly get to know your friends. Then a call came out of the blue from poor Greta inviting me to become a sentinel. Like you, I had never heard of them, but I jumped at the chance to join if only to get away from the turmoil that had overtaken my life. You basically know the rest."

Mike said, "I think you had a lucky escape from your so-called fiancé."

Amy replied with tears in her eyes, "You think you know people, but you have to experience a big problem together to really see them fully."

They fell into silence for a while.

"How do we attack the Infiltrator?" Amy asked.

"I wish I knew. The only location we have is in that tunnel and in truth I don't know if that is the only source."

"Still, I think it must help if we eliminate it," Amy said.

Noting that she was getting back to the Amy he had first met, lifted Mike's heart accordingly.

"Well, here we are," Mike said as they pulled into a caravan park. "Wait here and I will get us some accommodation."

Amy looked around at the site. It did not look too bad. The chalets seemed in good order at least from the outside.

"I would not like to spend too much time here, but if I have to, then spending it here with Mike makes it acceptable." She said to herself.

"Well, we have somewhere to stay," Mike said aloud as he waved a set of keys in the air.

They went to the caravan and stowed what little clothing they had.

"OK. Now that we are settled in, let's make a start on our plan of attack. Firstly, what will it take to put that electric tunnel out of action?" Mike said.

"We originally thought water might do it. Do you still think it will?" Amy asked.

"Getting the water there is the problem. We don't have hoses and connections. I think we have to look at other methods," Mike said.

"It needs power so maybe that's where we should concentrate our efforts," Amy said.

"The more I think about it, I am sure they would have more than one power source. They are too advanced to be at the mercy of local power cuts, etc. Also, there has to be a central point where all the broadcasting onto the net takes place and that is what we should look for," Mike replied.

"How?" Amy asked.

"Here's an idea. However powerful the Infiltrator is, it does not seem capable of moving around, otherwise why would it employ idiots like Mark. So, if we cause a blip to the tunnel power source, then it will think it is repairable and will send someone to check it out. We can then follow them and hopefully get closer to the heart of the beast," Mike said.

"Sounds good. How do we cause the blip?" Amy replied.

"Let's wait till we get there before we decide," Mike answered.

"Well, there is not a lot of daylight left so maybe we should call it a day and start fresh tomorrow," Mike said.

"I see that there are only single beds." Amy said, looking pointedly at Mike.

"One each," Mike lied.

Oh! With that, Amy picked up her clothes and went into the bedroom.

Mike thought to himself. *What is wrong with you turning down an invitation like that.*

Mike awoke with a hand on his shoulder. I am sure there is enough room in my bed," Amy said quietly.

Mike thought at first, he was dreaming, then realisation crept in and he slowly rose, lifted Amy into his arms, and carried her over to her bed.

Next morning, they had an early breakfast at a roadside cafe and then drove to the business park where they unloaded the equipment.

"These meters will locate the cables taking the power into the unit within the tunnel. We can then find an access point, cut the cables, and that will surely cause a blip."

Working steadily, Mike eventually found an inspection cover. He lifted the cover and with heavily insulated gloves on his hands he severed the cable. Their intense concentration on the cable route caused them to not see the man quietly looking out of the window of an adjoining unit and taking a keen interest in what they were doing.

"I think we can just hide in the car and wait for someone to turn up," Mike said.

The man watching picked up his phone, "You were right Master they have come back. What should I do?"

"How did they arrive?" The Infiltrator spoke sharply.

"By car," the watcher replied.

"Give me the registration number," again the Infiltrator barked the order.

The watcher gave the number.

"I am sending other units to you now, if the troublemakers leave, follow them and let me know where they are living, and I will take care of them there."

"What about the damage they have done?" The watcher asked.

"Do they think they can halt me by the isolating one of my power sources? I have more units than they could ever comprehend." The Infiltrator screamed down the phone. "Get it repaired immediately." The call ended.

God, it is touchy. If it has plenty of power sources then why does it need this one repaired so quickly, thought the watcher.

"Mike, I don't feel safe sitting in the car so close to the tunnel unit," Amy said with a worried look on her face.

"OK. Maybe you are right. We are a bit exposed. We will locate outside the business park, but where we can see the unit."

Mike started the car and started to drive away from the unit.

Looking back, Amy saw someone dash out of a unit and jump into a car.

"Mike we are being followed."

"Shit. If they know it is us then they will know the car registration number. We have to get rid of the car quickly."

"Where is the nearest shopping mall with a multilevel car park?" Mike added.

"Quick, turn right here then second left. It will lead us to Millbank Mall," Amy directed.

Mike got through the entrance barrier and accelerated up the ramp to the third floor and quickly swung into a parking space. They both jumped out of the car and avoiding the main exit, hid behind the emergency exit door, easing it open a crack so they could see the approach ramp to their floor.

A minute later, the car following them sped on to the third floor and screeched to a halt beside their parked car. They could see the driver wildly looking around. Not bothering to find a parking space he left his car such that it blocked their car in. He then jumped out and rushed towards the mall entrance.

Mike snuck across to his own car and filled a bag with electronic equipment then waved to Amy to join him as he proceeded to walk down the emergency stairs towards the exit.

"I think we are beaten," Amy said quietly as they walked down the stairs. "After all our trying, we are no further forward in finding the Infiltrator's location."

"It's not looking good but what will our lives be if we allow it to get away with everything we hold dear, not forgetting murder. I think we must have at least one more attempt to derail it so let's turn the tables on the latest one who is following us. Maybe we will learn something more about the Infiltrator." They turned and walked back up the stairs.

The man who was following them was on his phone

"You lost them. Why am I cursed with idiots?" screamed the Infiltrator. "Find them if you want to live." The call ended.

He turned towards his car still shocked at the Infiltrator's tirade. He did not see Mike until his free arm was jerked up his back. He dropped his phone and kicked out at Mike's legs. Amy strode up and kicked him violently between his legs. He dropped to the ground groaning. Mike finished the proceedings with a right-hand punch to the temple.

Mike went through the man's pockets and found a gun and the car keys. He unlocked the car, opened the rear door and dragged and lifted the unconscious man onto the back seat. He then got into the rear of the car and handed the car keys to Amy. "You drive. I will look after him if he regains consciousness."

There were people standing aghast, but no one interfered. Amy picked up the fallen phone, settled behind the steering wheel and accelerated down the exit ramp. Using Mike's parking ticket, they paid and exited the car park.

"People will phone this car's registration number to the police, so we only have a short time to extract information from him," Mike said, pointing to the unconscious man.

They drove into a wooded area and stopped.

The man had a dazed look of surprise. His eyes moved as he quietly looked around. His eyes narrowed as he saw Mike looking at him. His eyes then took in the fact that a gun, his own gun, was pointing directly at him.

"What do you want?" he asked. "I don't have any money."

"Don't insult us. We know who you work for and why you were following us," Mike spat out the words.

The man tried to ease himself up into a sitting position. Mike roughly pushed him back down.

"You should know I am quite willing to kill you, although knowing your master and if past experience is anything to go by then, it is more than likely it will do the job for me," Mike said firmly.

"What do you mean it will do the job for you?" The man asked.

"Have you asked what happened to your predecessor? I would be very careful with that phone," Mike said with a grim smile on his face.

"Phone! What is wrong with the phone?"

"You will find out when you become less than useful to your master," Mike replied.

The man looked puzzled and a bit scared.

"I know your game. You are just trying to scare me so I will give you information." The man said, again trying to sit up.

Mike put his hand out warning him to lie back. The man made a grab for Mike's arm. The report of the gun was deafening inside the car. The car door window shattered. The man fell back with his hands over his face in a protective stance.

"I warned you!" shouted Mike. "The next one will be in your head."

"Why are you threatening to kill me?" The man asked in a frighten voice. "All I was doing was following you."

Mike interrupted, "With a gun?"

"The Master said you were dangerous and that you killed the last person who was following you."

Amy leant over the car seat. What's your name?

"Joe," the man answered.

"Well Joe, you should know we did not kill Mark, who was your predecessor, the thing you call the Master killed him. It also killed three more of its helpers and three of our friends." She ended the statement with a sob and with tears in her eyes.

Joe looked shocked, "It is always threatening death, but I thought it was just bull."

"It is not bull. It is deadly," Mike said. "It has repeatedly tried to kill us, and you are the new conduit for a further attempt."

"Why is it so desperate to kill you?" Joe asked.

"We are interrupting its plans to take over the web among other things. The interruptions have been mainly by accident, but it suffers no interference. Hence we are on the run and three of our friends are dead."

"You are exaggerating. It could not take over the web," Joe said with a laugh.

"You think so? How did you get involved with it?" Mike asked.

Joe went quiet for a moment. "I was in a bit of trouble with the law and I was broke. It contacted me when I was in an internet café. It promised to get rid of the problem with the law, which it did, and then it put a lot of money into an account I gave it. All I had to do was follow you and give your location so that it could speak to you and clear up some misunderstandings."

"Yes, the misunderstanding is that we are still alive," Mike added.

"Does the fact that it could trace you, alter law enforcement documents and then pump money into an account, not give you an insight into its power?" Amy said.

"Of course. But to me that was a plus. I am no internet expert. Maybe anyone with programming skills could do it. I thought how lucky I was to have been chosen."

"So did poor Mark until that evil creature, or whatever it was, killed him," interrupted Amy.

"So, If I accept what you are saying what do you want from me?" asked Joe warily.

"How do you contact it?" asked Mike.

"With the telephone you have taken off me. However, there was something strange with the last few calls. I saw numbers come up as if they were made from normal phones and not the usual internet connection, so maybe your sabotage of the cable worked."

Mike's ears pricked up, "Could this be the weakness they had been waiting for?"

"Amy, let me have the phone," Mike exchanged the gun for the phone which Amy immediately pointed forcefully at Joe. He looked nervous.

Mike checked the numbers of the phones which had rang in. "Got you!" he shouted. "Now let's turn the tables on this Infiltrator."

They drove back to the mall. Mike turned to Joe who was lying on the back seat. "You can get out here. If you want my advice, don't contact it, and if you do, don't tell it you have failed. It will kill you. Go to your bank or wherever you have your money, withdraw it and disappear."

With that, Joe struggled up, opened the car door and ran into the mall.

Mike made a record of the numbers off Joe's phone then crushed it underfoot as he said, "Just in case the Infiltrator still has control of it." They then returned to their own car and then drove to an internet café that Mike had used previously.

"Don't worry," he said to Amy. "I never use my real name. It may track me down eventually but hopefully it will be too late."

Mike sat at the computer console and tracked down the identity of the telephones which had called the Joe's phone.

"It has been taking over the numbers of normal phones, but it is not as clever as it thought. It is not the only one who can break into a phone company system. I have been able to pinpoint where the calls were made from and they are all from one spot. We have the bastard."

"Where is it located?" Amy asked.

"Believe it or not it is located at the tunnel site."

"How did we miss it? Maybe we should look at it differently," Amy offered.

"You could be right. Maybe it is not a 'who' but a 'thing'," Mike answered.

"OK. But how could a 'thing' build that contraption you saw in the tunnel?" Amy asked.

"It seems to know the internet very well. It also seems to be able to move money freely so it could easily arrange for a business to build it," Mike answered.

"But how about the sophisticated equipment needed to infiltrate the internet?" Amy asked.

"You don't need sophisticated equipment. What you need are sophisticated programmes that will penetrate the internet," Mike answered.

"So, what was it you saw in the tunnel? You had not seen anything like it," Amy asked with a puzzled look on her face.

"I truly don't know. It could be the interface with something beyond our knowledge. But in truth I don't care as I am going to destroy it."

"OK. Plan?" Amy asked.

"I haven't got one," Mike answered with frown on his face.

"Can I again suggest water?" Amy asked.

"You can but we have the same old problem; how do we get the water into the building?" Mike replied.

"We don't, we let someone else to do it for us," Amy answered with a big smile on her face.

"OK. I am waiting," Mike said.

"We light a big fire in the building making sure it gets into the tunnel. Then we ring for the Fire Brigade."

Mike turned and hugged Amy, "Absolutely brilliant."

"Petrol, inflammable material and some type of fuse so we can get clear. That's the shopping list. So, let's go." Amy's excitement was bubbling.

"We need lots of materials and a big blaze to convince the Fire Brigade to put sufficient water into the tunnel to kill the Infiltrator off, therefore we cannot buy all of it at one place.

They will become suspicious and it will end up with us being charged with arson. It has to be done carefully."

"Hold on. Surely, we will be putting the firemen at risk. Electricity will travel up the stream of water coming from the hose and could possibly kill whoever is holding the hose," Amy said with a worried look on her face.

"Not if we make sure the electric cable is cut," Mike answered with a smile.

"Also, we need a van to carry all the material we require. I cannot afford to buy one, so we have to hire one," Mike said.

"Or steal one," Amy said with a laugh.

"You are encourageable," laughed Mike. "I would steal one, but we will need a number of trips so the chances of getting caught with a stolen van will increase exponentially. So unfortunately, we have to be honest and hire one."

"Let's get to it," Amy said.

They drove to a van-hire company and hired the van.

Mike said, "Give me a few minutes start with the van then you follow me in the car back to the caravan. We will rest up there and start the attack tomorrow."

"They are quite resourceful." The man driving the car following the van said.

"Yes, they are. So, hang back and make sure they don't see you," another man sitting in the back of the car said.

"What about the guy who followed them to the Car Park?" The man driving asked.

"He's been taken care of. He never made it out of the mall."

"Dead?"

"No, he is being spoken to."

The man driving grinned and asked, "Tell me again. Why don't we want to stop the thing corrupting the internet?"

When we found out what it was doing, we contacted a company working in the information field. They said it was a proverbial gold mine and they must have it at any cost. They are learning from it continuously. It is their gateway into infiltrating every system on the planet. When they have it, the

Russian Government's hackers will be small fry compared to them. Every system in the world will be open to them. Google, etc. will be at their mercy. It will make a fortune for all of us."

"If it's such a big deal so why did we not stop them from cutting the cable?" The driver asked.

"As I said they are resourceful, more than we gave them credit for, so due to our underestimation we lost them."

"I bet someone got their ear bent." The driver said with a laugh.

"Shut up and concentrate on your driving." The man responded sharply.

Oops. Touched a sore spot, thought the driver with a secret grin.

"We won't lose them again." The man in the back of the car muttered to himself grimly.

"Where have you been?" asked Mike. "I have been here in the caravan for over 30 minutes. I thought something terrible had happened to you."

"In a way it has," Amy replied. "Someone was following the van. They are parked outside the entrance to the site. I had to hang back, park some distance away, then scramble over fields to get here unseen."

"I don't know who they are, but what I do know is that I am fed up with running. I am going to find out who the hell they are. I still have the gun we took of the man at the mall. So, I am going to put them under a bit of pressure," Mike said angrily.

Mike left the caravan park on foot and crept around the perimeter until he came up to the parked car from the rear. He opened the driver's door and pulled the car keys out of the ignition switch.

"Who are you, and why are you following me?"

The driver went to loosen his seat belt saying, "You should know we are armed."

"Is your gun as big as this one," Mike said showing the driver his gun.

The driver slumped back in his seat and took his hands off the seatbelt catch.

"Now listen here," a man in the back of the car started to say.

Mike interrupted and snarled to the driver, "Tell him to shut up unless he is asked a question, or you will be the one to suffer."

"For God's sake shut up, you idiot!" The driver screamed at the man in the back.

The man in the back bristled. "Don't you dare talk to me like that," Mike interrupted him. "I will ask you once again. Who are you and why are you following me? Otherwise I will move this to the next level. You, at the back, start talking."

"You will regret this."

This was as far as he got before Mike aimed the gun at him.

"No," he squealed but his hands up to his face.

"We are employed by the government. We have been actively watching the thing you are trying to sabotage. We want it to continue until we have learnt all of its tricks."

"Well, I don't. It has caused the deaths of three people that I know of and I am going to stop it," Mike snarled.

"You will regret it," the man at the back said shakily. "There are forces at work which will swallow you up."

Something clicked in Mike's mind, "You don't work for the government. You are commercial and you don't care if it hurts people. You are after the Infiltrator's power for yourselves."

The silence from the two men was palpable.

"So how did you get onto it?" Mike added.

"I'm not telling you anything," the man at the back said.

"Let me guess. You are the contractors who built the little nest for it. You wondered what it was all about and started checking particularly as all the arrangements were done online. Somehow you found out it was manipulating the internet. Why did you bother checking on it; did it not pay you?"

"It paid us," the driver started to say.

"Shut up. Don't say another word!" the man in the back shouted.

Mike moved around the front of the car to the rear passenger's door. He opened it and entered the back of the car.

Passing the car keys to the driver he said, "Drive onto the caravan site and follow my directions."

"You can't keep us. We will be missed." The man alongside him said.

"Shut your mouth or I will shut it for you," Mike growled at him.

The man went silent.

Amy looked shocked when Mike pushed the two men into the caravan.

Mike handed her some money. "Take the car and purchase some long cable ties and some wide tape. I will look after these two idiots."

"Sit down," he said, waving the gun at the two men.

"You don't appreciate the damage you are doing. We all could learn a lot from this creature." The man from the back of the car said.

"You mean such as controlling people's lives? Well, I have news for you. It is not going to happen."

After an hour, Amy hurriedly brought the cable ties and tape into the caravan.

Mike handed her the gun.

"We can do this the hard way or the easy way. Get into the bedroom and lie on your stomachs on the bed. Hands behind your back. Amy, if they resist shoot one of them. Remember not in the head like last time."

Amy gave Mike a puzzled look, then quietly smiled as he winked at her.

"OK, are you sure you don't want them dead?" She replied, trying to sound disappointed.

Mike used the cable ties to secure their hands behind their back then using more ties secured their legs. He then bent their legs at the knees and tied the leg ties to the arm ties.

"You will regret this." Was as far as the man from the back of the car got before the tape went across his mouth.

"Well, they are not going anywhere now?" Mike said and waved for Amy to leave the bedroom.

"When they were out of earshot of the prisoners," Mike said.

"We are going to have to change our plans. We cannot leave them here indefinitely."

"So, what can we do?" Amy asked.

"Whatever it is, we have to do it quickly."

"Is there anything else which will destroy the Infiltrator other than water?" Amy asked.

"I am out of ideas. What about you?" Mike said with a grimace.

"How did it survive long enough to get help when we cut the cable?" Amy said out loud.

"It must have a backup system, batteries or a generator," Mike answered.

"Maybe we should attack the backup system," Amy offered.

Mike grabbed Amy and planted a kiss on her lips. "You are a genius."

Amy smiled happily and said, "I am going to come up with more ideas on a regular basis from now on."

"So, we now have to find the backup system," Mike said.

"It can't be far away from the Infiltrator's lair," Amy answered.

"If it is batteries, then there would be lots of them and they would need a considerable space and they would also have to be hidden away from interference. So, in all probability, they are underground which means there must have been an excavation similar to the lair. I wonder if our friends in the bedroom can shed any light on the location?"

Mike ripped the tape off the mouth of the man who had been in the back of the car.

The look he gave Mike was one of fear.

"You will pay for this," he said.

"Maybe," Mike replied. "But you will not be around to make me pay unless you give us what we want, so remember that."

"What now?" The man asked.

"What other work did you do for it?"

"Nothing." The man answered.

The man lying next to him started wriggling and nodding his head.

"Looks like your colleague has more sense than you."

Mike started to put the tape back onto the man's mouth.

"OK, OK. Two buildings down, we excavated and lined a cellar. The building above the cellar was rented out to a genuine company so we never got to see what was eventually put into the cellar. In fact, we have never seen what is in the cellar of the thing you are trying to destroy. We were just told to keep it safe."

"What's the name of the company occupying the building?"

"I forgot." The man replied.

The other man started wriggling again.

"Your friend most definitely has more sense than you. I will ask you once more. What is the name of the company occupying the building?"

"Forward Housing Development, or something like that."

"Thank you." Ignoring his protests, Mike stuck the tape back over the man's mouth.

He returned to the living room where Amy was sitting.

"The backup power source is located close to the Infiltrator. Now we have to find out how to get into that location."

"It is night time and dark outside so why not have a look at the building now." With that, they walked out to the car.

After parking the car at the entrance to the business park, Mike put the car keys on top of the rear wheel adding, "Just in case we get split-up." They entered the business park on foot.

Carefully they passed the location of the Infiltrator noticing the same amount of pseudo activity showing through the windows and approached the building possibly containing the power backup.

"It is not any different to most office buildings so it should be easy to break in," Amy said.

"The door could be alarmed so I think we have to look for a less obvious way in, so let's have a good look around," Mike said.

"They have a loading bay. I see they have padlocked the door. Amy stay here and look for any activity. I will get the cable cutter from the car; it should do the job."

Mike hurried back to the car.

Amy positioned herself in the shadows close to the loading bay, her senses at high alert as she scanned the area for any activity. Then she heard movement from the direction of the Infiltrator's building. It sounded as though someone was exiting the building through the loading bay. Footsteps approached. She pushed herself further into the shadows. Just as she thought she must be discovered, the person turned up the path at the side of the building and walked towards the front entrance.

She prayed quietly to herself for Mike to either come back from the car later or quietly.

She jumped when a hand touched her.

"It's me," Mike said quietly.

"You nearly gave me heart attack," Amy whispered, her heart pounding.

"Sorry, but I could not approach any other way."

"I take it you saw the person leave the other building?" Amy asked.

"Yes, I was lucky I was walking in a darkened section when he came out of the building," Mike said quietly, then added, "It looks as though they check-up on the backup system so we are going to have to be extra careful. We will wait until he leaves as I doubt, he is going to stay all night."

They snuggled down as best they could in the darkened part under the loading bay.

Neither Mike nor Amy saw or heard the group of men approaching them. They certainly felt the shock of the Taser as it hit them.

Mike regained consciousness. He looked around the room. It was difficult to decide if it was a hospital room or a hotel room. He sat up on the bed surprised he was not bound. *At least I am still alive,* he thought.

The door to the room opened and a man walked in.

"You have been a very naughty boy." The man said with a smile on his face.

"Who are you and where is Amy?" Mike asked rising to his feet.

"Firstly, she is safe and being well-looked after. Secondly, my name is Philip. Thirdly, don't try anything stupid as there are plenty of people outside that door."

"Well Philip, why am I here and what gives you the right to Taser us and by the looks of it, imprison us here?" Mike asked angrily.

"We belong to a department who can do anything we like to people acting against the best interests of the country," Philip said with the smile still on his face.

"We were not acting against the countries interest. If anything, we were protecting the country from the rapacious actions of a murderous Infiltrator," Mike answered sharply.

"Yes, and you were doing too good a job. We had to stop you from possibly eliminating the intruder before we had completed our investigation and analysis," Philip answered.

"If you have been investigating it why have we not seen or sensed you?" Mike asked warily.

"You are not the only one who has the ability to electronically track what is going on. We have been onto this Infiltrator, as you call it, for best part of a year," Philip said smiling smugly.

"Then why did you let it kill those three innocent people, or four if you count its minion?" Mike asked angrily.

The smile left Philip's face. "So, you want the facts. So, I will tell them to you. You caused the deaths of those people. They were isolated but unharmed until you interfered. In fact, the only time it had acted in a life-threatening manner was when it exploded your computer. Yes, we know about that incident. So, before you throw blame around, I suggest you look at yourself."

Mike sank back and sat on the bed; he was astounded. He then turned and snarled at Philip. "I tried to save those people from a trapped none-life and if you knew so much about what was going on why did you not stop the Infiltrator before it could harm them. No, you put your own interests first so do not try to put all the blame onto me. My involvement was based on helping them, yours was criminal neglect. An independent voice would know where the real blame lies."

Philip reared back in shock at the outburst.

"There will be no independent voice, as you call it, and I think we are done for the moment." With that, Philip turned and left the room, locking the door behind him.

"What is going on here?" Mike asked himself.

Philip walked in to his boss' office. "Hi Simon, I have just left the prisoner Mike. He is going to be a handful. It will take more than threats to make him walk away."

"OK. We will use the girl to make him drop this vendetta," Simon said.

Suddenly, Mike remembered the two men tied-up in the caravan.

He banged and kicked the door of the room.

A voice shouted through the door, "Keep that up and you will get another dose of the Taser."

Mike shouted through the door, "Listen. There are two men tied-up in a caravan and because you Tasered me I don't know how long they have been there. Their lives could be in danger. You have to get someone to release them!"

"Tell me another one." The voice said laughing.

"Get me Philip now, you idiot, or by God I will make sure you pay for your stupidity."

"What's going on?" Mike heard Philip's voice.

Mike shouted, "Philip, I need to talk to you!"

The door opened and Philip and another man walked into the room.

"Who is he?" Mike asked.

"That is none of your business," Philip said sharply.

"If he is the idiot who was standing outside the door then get rid of him because he is nearly responsible for two people's death," Mike spat the words out.

"I thought he was playing tricks." The man said.

"OK. Leave now, we will discuss this later," Philip said pointedly.

The man left with a venomous look at Mike.

"So, what is this about two people's death?" Philip asked.

Mike explained the situation at the caravan site and asked that Philip arrange for their release.

"Consider it done. But one good turn deserves another. Please remember that." Philip then left the room again, locking the door.

A little later, there was a kick on the door and a voice said, "You will pay for that little episode. Count on it."

"Open the door now and make me pay. Unless you are waiting for help?" Mike spoke through the door hoping his voice did not carry too far.

"Wait until this place becomes quieter, then we will see how tough you are," the voice replied.

Got you, thought Mike.

Mike got into bed and slowly adjusted the bedding such that when he got out it would still look as if someone was sleeping in it. He knew that there was certainly a camera in the room watching him. But he surmised that if the idiot agent was going to assault him then it would be switched off.

A few hours later, Mike heard the key quietly turn in lock. Mike quickly rose and positioned himself behind the door.

The man burst into the room and aimed a Taser at the supposed body in the bed.

"This is what you are going to get for trying to make me look foolish. Now get yourselves out of bed."

"I don't have to make you look foolish. You do a good job yourself," Mike said as he moved quickly towards to the man.

The man turned with a shocked look on his face. Mike punched him hard in the jaw. As he went down, Mike grabbed the Taser from his hand and let him have the full voltage.

He dragged the now unconscious man further into the room. He took the official badge off the man's coat noting he was called William. He then searched the man's pockets and found car keys, a mobile phone and a small amount of cash. Leaving the room, he locked the door with the keys which were still in the lock. He then noticed that there was a sign saying 'Occupied' on the door. He started to walk slowly down the corridor looking and listening for any signs of Amy.

Two doors down from where he had been kept, he saw another 'Occupied' sign and wondered if he was that lucky.

After trying three or four keys, he found one that worked. Opening the door, he saw Amy lying on the bed. Hoping she was not unconscious he shook her. She awoke with a start, "Oh, Mike. What has happened to us? I thought I might never see you again." Tears filled her eyes.

"I am the proverbial bad penny. You will never get rid of me," he said as he hugged her close.

"We have to move I am sure we don't have much time."

They exited Amy's room carefully locking the door.

"Look as though I am escorting you," Mike said as he got a hold of her upper arm and pushed her forward.

As they approached the door leading to outside, a voice came from behind a desk. "What are you doing, leaving without signing out?"

"Sorry," Mike said. "A bit of an emergency. She has to go to hospital. Let me sign out."

"You're not William," was as far as he got before the Taser dropped him.

Once outside, they hurried to the car park with Mike continuously pressing the car key button.

After what seemed like an eternity, the lights flashed on a convertible car. They quickly got in and hurriedly drove away from the area.

They drove into a shopping mall car park and parked.

"What now?" Amy asked.

"I wish I knew," Mike replied.

"Irrespective of what those men said about monitoring the Infiltrator, I still think it is dangerous," Amy said.

"I feel the same. So maybe we should carry on with our plan to kill it," Mike said.

The mobile phone Mike had taken off the agent rang.

"Hello, this is Philip. You have been busy. You will be pleased to note that William has recovered. He wants to make your acquaintance again. Ha–ha." Mike turned the phone onto speaker so that Amy could hear what was being said.

"So, what do you want to talk about Philip other than trying to find our location?" Mike asked brusquely.

"Firstly, we have released the two men you tied up and persuaded them to forgive you and also to inform their company that they are not welcome in the race to gather the Infiltrator's secrets. As a payment for this generous act I want to ask you, note, not tell you, to desist from attacking what you have called the Infiltrator. We have it under control now and you would be doing your country a disservice if you damaged it," Philip said in a formal voice.

"What about all the damage it has done to people's lives, not only the one's it caused to die but the likes of Amy and to some extent myself who have lost their jobs have been made penniless and spent significant amounts of time in hiding. How are they going to feel if we just give up the fight?"

"We are now aware of these actions and we intended to compensate everyone. We will make sure Amy gets her job back and is financially compensated for all the problems that she has suffered. You also would be financially compensated, and we would also like to offer you the position of Coordinator for the changeover of what you call the Infiltrator's programmes to our system. What do you say?"

"I say I will let you know," Mike answered then ended the call.

"Do you think he is genuine?" Amy asked.

"I think he was trying to hold us on the phone. Someone must be on their way. So, we had better move our location."

Mike left the phone in the car and they both hurried across to a dark part of the car park and found a place behind a fence which gave them a view of the car.

Ten minutes later, a car screeched into the car park. Four men quickly got out. One dialled a number on his phone and the phone Mike had left in the car started to ring. The four men dashed across to the car and wrenched the doors open. They turned as one and began to slowly visually scan the car park. They then spread out and began to search the car park. After 30 minutes or so, they gave up and got back into their car and left the car park.

"So much for Philip's offer," Mike said angrily.

"Is there no one we can trust?" Amy asked quietly.

"I think the answer is no. So, if we cannot rely on their trust then we have to use fear."

"Sorry I am lost! I don't think we will ever be able to kill off the Infiltrator as they will be guarding it night and day," Amy said with resignation in her voice.

"I agree. But Philip said they are basically taking over from the Infiltrator. So, their computers must be duplicating its programmes. When that is done, they will switch off the Infiltrator and then kill it to prevent anyone else gaining its knowledge. Once this happens, they will totally rely on their own computers. This is their Achilles Heel. I am going to access their servers ASAP and plant a virus before they have enough of the Infiltrator's programme to prevent access. We will then have to hide until the changeover happens and then we will be in charge and it will be payback time."

"Do you know where their servers are?" Amy asked.

"Actually, I worked for the government for a few years and I am sure I know which department these guys work for."

"But can you get into their computers?" Amy asked.

"I can access their systems with my eyes closed," Mike answered with a smile.

"So, let's get to it," Amy said rising from their hiding place.

"So, it is back to the Business Park to pick up the car," Mike said as they walked towards the shopping mall.

"How will we pay for a taxi?" Amy asked.

"No problem, whenever I am getting into a dodgy situation, I always put my credit cards and some folding money in my socks. No one ever looks there," Mike answered smiling.

The taxi dropped them off close to the Business Park.

They picked up the car and drove away in order to put a few miles between them and anyone at the Infiltrator's location who was associated with Philip.

"Do you think we could return to the caravan to get my things?" Amy asked.

"We can get close to it and check if anyone's watching it," Mike replied.

They approach the caravan on foot. It was all in darkness which gave a small indication that maybe no one was there.

Mike said to Amy, "You stay here, and I will check it out."

He slowly and quietly found his way to the door. It was not locked. As he entered, he thought he heard deep breathing. Someone was asleep on one of the chairs.

Vagrant or enemy? Mike thought. *What choices do I have?* So, he aimed the Taser at it.

The person stiffened in the chair then their head rolled to one side.

Mike turned the light on. It was the same man he had tasered in the place where he had been confined. "Sorry William," he said.

Amy's head appeared around the doorway. "I saw the light and prayed you had turned it on. Goodness, who is that? Is he dead?"

"No, he is not dead. He is unconscious, so we better get what you want before he comes around as I really don't want to zap him again."

They gathered up what they wanted and left the caravan after turning out the light.

"I think we have to take a risk and return to my house. I have computers there which will enable me to easily get into Philip's servers," Mike said.

They left the car one street away from Mike's house and slowly walked past it carefully looking out for anyone observing the premises. It seemed clear.

They returned and scaled the rear fence. Mike got his spare key from its hiding place and they entered the house. Nothing stirred. I don't think we should turn the lights on so why don't we get some sleep and start the attack in the morning.

"I wondered when you would try to get me back into bed?" Amy said with a wicked smile on her face.

Mike kissed her and they both hurried upstairs.

When Amy awoke, her first thought was, *Where am I?* When the facts of the previous day filtered through, she then wondered where Mike was. Rising, she went down the stairs to find Mike sitting at a laptop computer at the same desk which had held the one destroyed by the Infiltrator. "You are up early," she said.

"Yup. Coffee is in the pot," he said nodding towards the kitchen.

Amy back into the room with two coffees. "Hope you don't want milk. It is off."

"Nope, black is fine."

"How is it going? Are you into their servers yet?" Amy asked looking over Mike's shoulder at the dizzying array of figures on the computer screen.

"No, I haven't tried yet. I am refining the virus. It has to be smart or they will detect it," Mike answered.

"How long will it take?" Amy questioned.

"I did a lot of work early this morning so I should be ready to inject it in an hour or so," Mike said turning and smiling at her.

"I will leave you to it," Amy said returning upstairs where she showered and changed her clothes.

Mike shouted up the stairs. "It's in. Now we just wait for Philip's mob to finish off the Infiltrator then we move against them."

"I assume we cannot stay here indefinitely. So where are we to go?" Amy asked.

"I have checked into a hotel under another of my pseudo names. I hope you don't mind a double room, Mrs Collins."

"Mrs Collins does not mind a double room. In fact, she would have been disappointed at any other arrangement."

"Good, let's get going," Mike said picking up two mobile phones from a draw.

"Your previous life must have been complicated if needed all this communication equipment? And won't they be able to trace those phones back to you?" Amy asked.

No, they are called Burner Phones. They have no reference back to me, and they will only be used once

They scaled the back fence and returned to the car.

After ten days they saw the television report of a huge explosion which had totally destroyed a building at a business park. Mike checked and found out it was the building which had housed the Infiltrator. The cause of the explosion had not been found.

"Now we will find out Philip's true intentions," Mike said to Amy as they sat in their hotel room.

They got in the car and drove out into the countryside so their hotel location could not be traced from the phone signal.

"How will you contact Philip?" Amy asked.

"I noted his number when he rang me on William's phone."

"Hello Philip. Mike calling."

"You are very elusive," Philip replied. "Where are you located?"

"Firstly Philip. We are not stupid so don't try to keep us talking while you try to locate us. Just answer a few questions," Mike said firmly.

"Fire away," Philip said.

"We did not attack the Infiltrator as requested. So how about your promise?" Mike asked.

"What promise was that?" Philip asked with a laugh.

"When you said you were going to recompense us for all the problems caused by the Infiltrator."

"No, we are not going to recompense you. We were never going to recompense you, and by the way, we found and neutralised the virus you put on our servers. Goodbye."

Philip ended the call.

"You heard all that. So, onto the next stage," Mike said to Amy grimly.

"What next stage? They have found the virus," Amy replied anguished.

"They found one virus. I put three onto their servers," Mike said with a smile.

Mike threw the mobile phone out of the car window as they drove back to the hotel.

Back at the hotel, Mike started the second virus.

Two days later, there was a message plastered all over the newspapers and television. "Would Infiltrator Mike please contact Philip?"

They drove out to a different location but still in the countryside. Mike got out the second Burner phone.

"Hello Philip. Mike calling."

"You bastard," Philip was almost spitting blood, "Do you realise what you have done?"

"Absolutely. But it could have been worse."

"What do you want?" Philip spat the words.

"You will put £10 million pounds into this account. Take this number down. Mike then read off a number. Got it?"

"I have got it, but do you think you can blackmail us?" Philip shouted.

"Yes," Mike said. "If you put in within 24 hours, I will neutralise the virus. If you don't, I will leave it operating. Also, there is another virus there. If you come after us or interfere with us in any way, I will active it and the programme will die. I will not be contacting you again. The decision is yours." Mike ended the call.

"I thought we were going to kill the programme. It sounds as though you are just in it for the money," Amy said with horror written on her face.

"I am in it for the money but only as recompense and protection. I am still going to kill the programme. I am going to be as devious as they have been. I think they will hunt for us in an attempt to recover the money. But when I kill the programme, the hunt for us could end up being fatal. So, I want to make sure both of us are financially strong enough to hide completely. It won't be easy, and it won't be cheap."

"Oh, thank goodness. You had me worried for a moment," Amy said with relief written on her face.

"Have you got a passport?" Mike asked.

"Yes, I have. The Infiltrator informed the Passport Office that I had died, and they therefore cancelled my passport. When I got isolated, I went to the passport people, proved I was alive and eventually got a new one. I have kept it close ever since," Amy said tapping her stomach.

"Good, because we are leaving the country tonight."

"May I ask where we are going?"

"I have told them to put the money into a Swiss bank so they will expect us to go there. But any money in that account is immediately transferred to the Cayman Islands and that is where we are going."

"When are we going?"

"Hopefully tomorrow, after I have check to see if the money has been transferred. Then we will start travelling."

"Which airport?"

"We will be flying, but not from a UK airport. It would be too easy to track us. We will take the Eurostar train to France and disappear for a while. Then travel to Cayman where we will divide the money 50-50."

"How about wrecking the programme?" Amy asked questioningly.

"As promised, I will cancel virus No. 2 when the money has been released. This will give us a breathing space. Once we are out of the country, I will activate virus No. 3 and kill it for two reasons. It deserves to die for the harm it has caused. Also, once they get to use it properly, they could reclaim the money easily. So please believe me it is going to die."

The money was transferred. They travelled to France and that is where Mike killed the programme. They succeeded in getting to Cayman and divided the money equally then left for pastures new.

Although both were financially independent, they stayed together under new names.

Philip is still looking for them.

The End